TWICE UPON A TIME
and other
NORTH BUCKS TALES

by
JOHN HOUGHTON

The
Book
Castle

First published October 1998
by
The Book Castle
12 Church Street
Dunstable
Bedfordshire LU5 4RU

ISBN 1 871199 09 3

Computer typeset by Keyword, Aldbury, Hertfordshire.
Printed by Progressive Printing (UK) Ltd., Leigh-on-Sea, Essex.

TWICE UPON A TIME
and other North Bucks Tales

These fifteen stories are tales of fiction with a touch of fact. But the places are all real and are all to be found in North Bucks.

Some of the people who appear here were real historical characters . . . Sir Edmund Verney for example, who lost his life at the Battle of Edgehill in 1642. And John Bunyan, the travelling tinker, who wrote 'Pilgrim's Progress'. And Thomas Adams of Swanborne, who was murdered 'on Liscombe ground' near Soulbury in 1626.

But all the other characters who appear in these pages are imaginary. And any likeness to actual persons is coincidental.

ABOUT THE AUTHOR

John Houghton was born in
Eastbourne in 1916. After graduating
at Durham University he was
ordained in 1939 and was Curate at
Wolverton (1939–1942). From 1942 to
1973 he served in Northern
Rhodesia/Zambia and was awarded
the Zambian Order of Distinguished
Service in 1966. He is a Canon
Emeritus of Lusaka Cathedral. He
retired in 1983 and lives in Bletchley.

The Author

Unlike the present volume, his
recent books have been concerned
with social history in the four
adjoining counties of Beds and Bucks, Northants and Herts.
They are:

'Murders & Mysteries, People & Plots'
'Eccentrics & Villains, Hauntings & Heroes'
'Myths & Witches, Puzzles & Politics'
Manors & Mayhem, Paupers & Parsons'
Historic Figures in the Buckinghamshire Landscape'

Photographs with the initials NK are by Norman Kent. Those
with the initials JH are by the Author.

CONTENTS

Page

ONE .... Twice Upon A Time 7

TWO .... Seen Moreton Lately? 11

THREE .... What the Window Cleaner Saw 19

FOUR .... Clerical Error 29

FIVE .... Jammy Strikes Again 34

SIX .... The Big Tickle 38

SEVEN .... If Only He Had Waited 44

EIGHT .... Jeux Sans Frontières 49

NINE .... Diddled By A Diddicoy 55

TEN .... Those That Take To The Sword 60

ELEVEN .... The Hand Of War 66

TWELVE .... A Fence Taken 72

THIRTEEN .... The Lamp 76

FOURTEEN . The Great Train Robbery – Mark Two 80

FIFTEEN .... The Turn Of The Century 85

ILLUSTRATIONS

Picture   Page

1. The Author 4

2. 350 years later, and 3,500 miles away, history repeated itself. (Photo: Norman Kent) 10

3. Should he throw the body in the canal? (Photo: The Author) 13

4. The Fire Brigade could do little to save it. (Photo: The Author) 17

5. It was a bitter winter in 1192 at Bradwell Abbey. . . 30

6. Father Abbot went over again to the Scriptorium. . 31

7. 'I've been there', said Lofty Prescott. 'It's a real tourist attraction'. (Photo: The Author) 36

8. 'John Bunyan was a Diddicoy'. 56

9. Wina Mulenga, in Africa, read all about Bridego Bridge. (Photo: Norman Kent) 81

10. The lorries and trucks were hidden in the bush. (Photo: The Author) 83

ONE

Twice Upon A Time

Johan Adams was a lecturer in English Literature at a College in Leonardtown, one of the delightful small towns in the State of Maryland in the USA. He was nothing if not a traditionalist. Johan was his Christian name and he relished the thought that there had been a Johan in the family as far back as anyone could trace. If people called him John he never failed to correct them. 'It's not John, it's Johan' he insisted. And because he was after all a lecturer in English Literature he would usually add: 'He that filches from me my good name robs me of that which not enriches him and makes me poor indeed'.

His sturdy traditionalism went further than just defending the odd spelling of his Christian name. He loved history in general and doted on family genealogy in particular. Truth to tell, he could be pretty boring on the subject and his friends did their best to steer him away from it. Only his father, Thomas Adams, shared his interest and enthusiasm. Between them they had researched the Adams family history back for ten genera-tions – no mean feat in a country as young as the USA. Their research had monopolised their spare time for years and nearly every vacation was devoted to it. When Thomas Adams, Johan's father, lost his wife their search intensified, Thomas finding solace as a widower in his study of the Adams family history.

So together Thomas and Johan Adams, father and son, traced their ancestors back through the generations. They could tell you what Adams menfolk had done in the two World Wars, in the American Civil War, and in the American War of Independence. And before that they could tell you of Adams involvement in the very earliest New England settlements in the 17th century. And in every one of the ten generations that spanned this period they had found a Johan Adams.

Their crowning achievement was the discovery that among the colonists who came from England in 1634 to make the very first settlement in Maryland there had been a Johan Adams. 'You should write a book on it' said Thomas Adams, and his son agreed. But Johan also pointed out that it would make a much better book if it could cover not only the ten generations of the Adams in New England but also trace the Adams back in *old* England as well. 'Tell you what we'll do' Johan said to his father, 'I've got a Sabbatical starting at the end of the year. We'll go over to England where the first Johan Adams came from and work back from there'.

So they made plans for their trip to England – a trip Thomas was destined never to make. For one night, on a lovely autumn evening, as he was crossing the common half a mile from home, he was set on by muggers who battered him to death and stole his watch and wallet.

So sickened was Johan by this that he was tempted to abandon all thought of the trip to England or the writing of the book. But then he had second thoughts. 'By God, I'll do it' he told himself. 'It'll be the old man's memorial. I'll do it for him'.

So Johan Adams came to England on his Sabbatical and settled into lodgings off the Marylebone Road. He spent days on end in the British Museum Reading Room, at the Library of the American Embassy, and at the Headquarters of the Society of Genealogists. He delved deep into Manorial Rolls and Records and became expert on the differences between Court Leet, Court Customery and Court Baron.

So there came the day when his search led him to the village of Swanborne in North Bucks. He had evidence enough now to hope that he would find what he most wanted – proof that it was from here that Johan Adams had gone to join that first group of colonists who had sailed across the sea to set up the first settlement in Maryland in 1634. And he was not disappointed. For there in the chancel floor of Swanborne church he found a brass. His heart quickened as he read its inscription:

'Here lyeth buried ye bodie of Thomas Adams
of this parish yeoman & Freeman of London
whoe had to wife Elizabeth and by her 4 children
viz. Robert and Thomas, Alice and Johan'

So there it was, and the twentieth century Johan Adams from the USA saluted his namesake of 350 years ago. But the inscription continued and he read on. As he did so he caught his breath, for the brass memorial to Thomas Adams went on to say:

'Hee departed this life ye 17 of October 1626'

And then there followed this verse:

'Behold in him the fickle state of man
which holie David likened to a span
In prime of youth by bloudie thieves was slaine
in Liscombe Ground his blood ye grasse did staine.
O cruel death–yet God turns all to best
for out of misery hee is gone to rest.'

'Twice upon a time' thought Johan Adams. 'My father, Thomas Adams, was mugged and murdered on Leonardtown Common this year, and here, 350 years before, and 3,500 miles away, this Thomas Adams met the same fate "in Liscombe Ground".'

And because, after all, he was lecturer in English Literature, Johan Adams found himself saying aloud in the empty Swanborne church:

'–or sign that they were bent
by paths coincident
on being twin halves
of one August event.'

9

HERE LYETH BVRIED Y BODIE OF THOMAS ADAMS
OF THIS PARISH YEOMAN, AND FREEMAN OF LONDON,
WHOE HAD TO WIFE ELIZABETH &BY HER 4 CHILDREN
VIZ ROBERT AND THOMAS ALICE AND IOHAN HEE
DEPARTED THIS LIFE Y 17 OF OCTOBER 1626.
Behold in him the fickle state of man
Wch holie dauid likened to a span
In prime of youth by bloudy Theues was slaine
In Liscombe ground his blood y grasse did staine
O cruel death yet God turnes all to best
For out of misery hee is gone to rest

350 years later, and 3,500 miles away, history repeated itself. NK.

TWO

Seen Moreton Lately?

God knows, he hadn't meant to kill Moreton. It had been such a stupid quarrel about so trivial a matter. But they both had such a low tolerance threshold and both operated on the shortest of fuses. So what began as a difference of opinion soon produced raised voices and angry gestures in the upstairs study. Moreton had flung out of the room and Wainwright stormed after him. They confronted each other on the landing, and the argument reached a crescendo. Both were shouting, neither listening to the other. Finally, seeking to drive home his point, Wainwright thumped Moreton on the chest, and Moreton had fallen backwards down the long oak staircase, with sickening thuds as he bounced from step to step, and finally landed in a heap in the hallway.

Wainwright rushed down the stairs, calling Moreton's name. He turned him over, felt his pulse and put an ear to Moreton's chest. But in his panic he couldn't decide whether it was Moreton's heartbeat he was hearing or his own. He sat back on his heels, staring at the wall, thinking furiously. It was late at night, and the house at the end of its long driveway was isolated – its nearest neighbour a quarter of a mile away. The curtains were drawn, and they were alone in the house,, Wainwright and the dead Moreton. Wainwright stayed where he was for several minutes, forcing himself to be calm. He must think what to do. He tested the body for pulse and heartbeat again, and this time thought he knew for certain that Moreton was dead. Fighting his panic, Wainwright tried as calmly as he could to make a plan. In that autumn of 1926, eight months after his wife's death, Wainwright had become something of a recluse, living alone in the old house, and managing tolerably well to look after himself. Mrs Turner cycled in from the village once a week on Fridays to give the house what she called 'a good going over'. Apart from that, Wainwright had little contact with the outside world. He had no friends, or even acquaintances, in the village of Billington, nor in nearby Leighton Buzzard. It was there that he did his shopping most weeks and sometimes had a meal out. And he used Leighton Buzzard Station for his occasional trips to London.

His renewed contact with Moreton had come about by chance. They had met by accident at Foyles Bookshop a few months ago, and the coincidence that Moreton, too, had recently been widowed, made something of a bond between them. Years before, in the closing months of the war, they had known each other in the army, and hadn't liked each other. But after that chance meeting in 1926, the curious parallels of their circumstances had overcome such antipathy. They had met once or twice for a meal in London, Wainwright going up by train from Leighton Buzzard, and Moreton coming in by Green Line coach from his lonely house at Godalming.

Such meetings hadn't given either of them much pleasure, and Wainwright would gladly have dropped Moreton and forgotten all about him. But then, two days ago, Moreton had telephoned, asking if he could come over to Billington to see Wainwright. He wouldn't say on the phone why he wanted to come, only insisting that it was urgent. Reluctantly Wainwright had agreed. It was settled that he would meet Moreton off the train at Leighton Buzzard at 6pm that Wednesday, and drive him back from Billington to Leighton Buzzard Station later that night for his return journey.

But now Moreton would never make that return journey. He now lay dead at the foot of Wainwright's staircase, and Wainwright's brain was frantically trying to decide what to do with the body. He so seldom had any visitors, and Mrs Turner was not due until Friday. He had, therefore, over twenty-four hours to carry out any plan he could come up with. But his instinct told him that delay would be fatal. He must get rid of the body at once, in the remaining hours of darkness that night. But how?

Should he throw the body into the Grand Union Canal, little more than a mile from his house? It wouldn't be the first body to be found in the canal – every year bodies were recovered from it somewhere along its length – and surely this would be taken as yet another suicide.

Or should he dump the body in one of the several deep gravel pits outside Leighton Buzzard? They were almost as near as the canal. But he dismissed them almost as soon as he thought of them. Too many people worked at the gravel pits. The body would be discovered that much sooner, and, he

Should he throw the body in the canal? JH.

13

thought, it was far less likely to be taken as suicide.

Or should he throw the body from a bridge over the main railway line? No – he rejected all three – canal, gravel pit, and railway line – because each would necessitate transporting the body over public highways and risk being seen.

A desperate new plan occurred to him. He would carry the body up on to the road that passed the end of his driveway and dump it there. Then he would fetch his own car and deliberately drive over the body, leaving it there for someone else to find, the supposed victim of a hit-and-run accident. Yes, that's what he's do – he could see no flaws in the plan.

So, made breathless both by exertion and fear, he carried the body in the darkness, fireman's lift fashion, along his drive to the road. Leaving it there, he ran back to his house, backed his bull-nosed Morris out of his garage, and drove it up his drive. He did this without switching on even his sidelights. As he prepared to turn out of his drive on to the road where he had dumped the body, he was tempted to close his eyes, not relishing what he knew he had to do. But he dismissed such squeamishness and drove on the last few yards.

But the roadway was empty. There was NO body!

He stopped the car, put it into reverse, and backed it a few yards. He even risked switching on his lights for a moment – but they showed only empty roadway, AND NO BODY!

Frantic now, he stopped the car and got out. He stared up the road, went first to one ditch and then to the other, looked over the hedges on both sides, and still there was NO BODY! 'But I put it there only minutes ago' he told himself, 'and he was dead – I checked and double-checked it'.

Panic really seized him then. He rushed back to the car, reversed it, and sped up the drive and into his garage. He locked the garage, ran into the house, and locked and bolted his front door. He was in a cold sweat, shaking with apprehension. With trembling fingers he poured himself a drink from the decanter on the sideboard.

All this happened on that Wednesday evening, in

mid-October 1926. Thursday came, and no developments. Friday came, and with it Mrs Turner – everything was as usual – no news, no alarms, and no developments.

And then came Saturday, and there *was* a development. It came just before midnight in the shape of a telephone call. The voice, which Wainwright didn't recognise, simply said 'SEEN MORETON LATELY?' And then the caller had hung up. That was all – just a voice saying: 'SEEN MORETON LATELY?', and then the click as the phone was replaced.

Wainwright passed a miserable and worried Sunday. Then, in Monday morning's post came a postcard. On it was written in capitals: 'SEEN MORETON LATELY?'. No signature and an indecipherable postmark.

After that it went on – sometimes a phone call, often in the middle of the night, with the caller simply saying: 'SEEN MORETON LATELY?'. And two or three times a week a postcard in the mail, post-marked in widely scattered towns, each card simply posing the questioon: 'SEEN MORETON LATELY?'. Those three words, written or spoken, began to haunt Wainwright.

After three weeks of this his nerves were in tatters. It couldn't go on like this – he had to do something to resolve the tension, and to settle the question: was Moreton alive or dead? With part of his mind Wainwright was sure Moreton *was* dead – he had checked the body so thoroughly. In that case, who moved the body? And what did that unknown person intend to do about it? Blackmail seemed the obvious answer. But if Moreton *wasn't* dead, then obviously it was he who was telephoning and sending the postcards. But why? And for how long would this persecution continue?

Wainwright came to a decision. He would go to Godalming and see for himself whether Moreton was there. He felt better for the decision – any action would be better than none after the torment of the past three weeks. He packed a bag, intending to go to Godalming and to book into some hotel or boarding-house there and to keep watch on Moreton's house. First he must let Mrs Turner know he was going away.

He walked into the village to her cottage, but got no reply to his knock. Her door opened to his touch and he went in. He would leave a note for her. Looking round the tidy sitting room for something on which to scribble his note, his eye caught sight of some postcards on the mantlepiece. He took them down, amazed when he saw that all of them, ready stamped for mailing, were addressed to him. All of them bore that damnable question: 'SEEN MORETON LATELY?'

Before he could begin to make sense of this unexpected development, Mrs Turner came in, with a basket of washing she had been taking from the line in her back garden. She saw the cards in his hand and flushed with embarrassment. In a torrent of words she told him the cards belonged to her son Jack – that she didn't know what they meant, that she had asked him over and over about them, and that he had told her to mind her own business. Jack Turner was a long-distance lorry driver (that explains the postmarks, thought Wainwright) and she was expecting him back that evening. Telling her sternly that she must send Jack up to the house as soon as he returned, Wainwright went home – the trip to Godalming postponed at least for the present.

An embarrassed but truculent Jack drove up to the house in his little Austin Seven later that evening and was was soon telling his tale. Three weeks ago, he said, he had been driving his Baby Austin along the road at the end of the drive. He was driving without lights because he was on his way to do a spot of poaching in Woburn Park. 'But I got the shock of my life – I nearly ran into a man sitting in the roadway. He was obviously in trouble, but I couldn't make up my mind whether he was mad or drunk or both. He told me he must get to Leighton Buzzard urgently to catch a train, and asked me for a lift. But when we got to the station, he didn't get out of the car at once. He asked me whether I would like to earn £5 a week for a month. He said all I had to do was to post some cards from different towns three times a week. So that's what I've been doing. He sent me the postcards in an envelope and so far he's

The Fire Brigade could do little to save it. JH.

sent me a fiver three times. I expected one more fiver when I posted those last three cards you've got there.'

Wainwright interrogated him thoroughly. Jack swore he knew nothing of who the stranger was, or why he was engaged on this strange exercise. All he had cared about was that he would get £20 for virtually no work at all.

Wainwright let him go at last and sat pondering what he should do next. It was clear that Moreton was getting his own back and making Wainwright pay for the accident on the stairs. But was that the whole story? Would there be more to follow when the month of phone calls and postcards was over? The more he thought about it the angrier Wainwright became. Next day he left for Godalming, not even bothering this time to let Mrs Turner know or to leave her the key. He would settle Moreton's hash once and for all.

And settle it he did. When Moreton's house caught fire in Godalming in late November 1926, the Fire Brigade could do little to save it. Its thatched roof was well ablaze when they arrived. Moreton's charred body was found inside. The Police were convinced it was arson, but could find no one to charge.

But the most puzzling feature of the case was the message they found scrawled on a paper pinned to the garden gate. It said:

'SEE ONLY ONE RAT MELT'.

They never did discover what that meant.

But miles away, in the village of Billington near Leighton Buzzard, the respectable Mr Wainwright could have told them it was an anagram of:

'SEEN MORETON LATELY?'

THREE

What The Window Cleaner Saw

Fred Briggs was whistling while he worked. He usually did. Those who knew him well could tell from his choice of tunes what sort of mood he was in. Today he was obviously happy – his rendition of 'Do you ken John Peel' showed that. And why not? It was a bright and sunny day, with more than a touch of spring in the air. It marked the end of six weeks of misery, of snow, frosts and biting east winds. Those six weeks had not been kind to window cleaners, and Fred's repertoire of mournful tunes had been severely tested.

Now it had all suddenly changed. The wind was from the west and spring seemed imminent. So Fred Briggs was saluting the change with his 'John Peel'. And he had a second reason to be content this morning. Much of his window cleaning business was domestic, and that meant, very often, having to call back at the houses in the evening to get paid. But he had a few contracts for larger buildings; for these he could rely on being paid on the spot. He was on his way to one such building this morning – Albion House.

Albion House was no sky-scraper. It was a modest three-storied block consisting entirely of lock-up offices. For Fred Briggs it was an attractive contract. He called there every three weeks, took the whole day to clean its windows, and got paid in cash by the Caretaker Manager at the end of the day.

He finished the ground floor windows first. Then he made a start on the second floor. 'John Peel' had by now been replaced in turn by 'Come lasses and lads' and 'Widdecombe Fair'. Fred wasn't one for modern rubbish – the songs he'd learned at school were good enough for him. When he moved his ladder to tackle the windows of Room 24 he was into 'Bobby Shafto'. But 'Bobby Shafto' froze on his lips when he looked through the window of Room 24. Lying on the floor in the middle of the room was a body. Fred stared at it for a moment, and then hastily descended his ladder and went in search of Mr White, the Caretaker Manager. Together they went up the stairs to the second floor, but the door of Room 24 was locked. Back in his cubbyhole Mr White phoned the Police.

The Constable came some seven minutes later. He climbed Fred's ladder to see for himself. 'Haven't you got a key for that door?' he called down to White. 'No, I haven't. I've got keys to all the others, but the chap who rents that room has changed the lock and wouldn't give me a spare key.'

'Who is he, and is that him lying there?'

'Yes, that's him. He's James Torvil. But shouldn't we break in? He may not be dead.' The Constable agreed, and proceeded to break the window. He climbed in, and the other two mounted the ladder and followed him through the window into the room.

'Don't touch anything,' said the Constable, and he pointed to something they hadn't been able to see from the ladder – a revolver in the dead man's hand. They could also now see the wound in his temple.

'Who is this James Torvil – What does he do?'

'He's an Inquiry Agent.'

'A private detective you mean?'

'I suppose so.'

'Well, leave everything as it is. It's obviously suicide. I'll go back to the Station and make a report.'

The Constable turned to go back to the window. His foot

moved something on the floor and he stooped to see what it was. It was a key. Picking it up, he went over to the door and inserted it in the lock.It turned easily. So the three men left by the stairs, the Constable locking the door of Room 24 behind him.

Detective Inspector Nisbet let himself into the room and the Police Surgeon joined him there. While the Doctor examined the body, the detective looked round the room. It was a bright, tidy office and suggested that its occupant was a methodical man. There was a large knee-hole desk, with a swivel chair behind it, a couple of other chairs, a filing cabinet and a cupboard. On the desk, a portable typewriter, a telephone, and a small stationery rack. A mat covered part of the floor which was otherwise polished.

Nisbet tried the desk drawers. All but one were locked. The only unlocked one contained nothing but a paper-punch, a stapler, and similar office gadgets. He tried the cupboard and filing cabinet. Both were locked.

'Any keys in his pocket, Doctor?'

The Doctor felt in the dead man's pockets and produced a key-ring.

'Thanks. Better let me have anything else in his pockets. Then you can take him away when you're ready.'

A wallet, a small diary, a man's purse and a couple of pens were found in Torvil's pockets. The Doctor called in two men who had been waiting with the ambulance downstairs and together they carried the body down and it was driven away to the mortuary.

'Wonder why he committed suicide?' thought Nisbet, as he made a start on the desk. The contents of the drawers told him nothing. He found Torvil's cheque book, paying-in book, and bank statements. He glanced quickly through these. Obviously they would have to be gone into more thoroughly, but in the meantime he saw nothing in them to suggest a reason for suicide. The cupboard yielded nothing at all of interest. Its contents were mostly stationery, with one shelf given over to a little crockery and the wherewithall for making tea and coffee.

That left the filing cabinet, a single-drawer affair which sat on top of the cupboard. It contained only about a dozen and a half files, the suspense variety, each one with a coloured tag. Torvil's methodical mind was in evidence here. White-tagged files clearly concerned Torvil's own affairs — Income Tax papers, household accounts and the like. A couple of green-tagged files looked as if they concerned Torvil's hobbies – one was given over to photography, and the other to angling. The remaining files, about a dozen of them, all had blue tags, and each one bore a name.

Nisbet took the blue-tagged files over to the desk, and settled down to study them one by one. After an hour of this he was no wiser. Nothing in them suggested any reason why Torvil should take his own life. On the contrary, he was impressed by the dead man's efficiency. Each file concerned one case handled by the private detective. Some of the cases were complete – others were clearly still in progress. They ranged from matrimonial cases to tracing missing persons, and from debt collecting to insurance probes.

A knock on the door interrupted his reverie. It was White, the building's manager.

'Everything alright, Mr Nisbet? Anything I can do for you?'

'Yes. Tell me about Torvil. How long's he been here? Where did he come from? Any family?'

'He's been here about a year. Don't know where he was before, except I do know he was working abroad somewhere. No family that I know of – he certainly lived alone.'

'OK, thanks. I'll lock up here when I finish, and look in to see you on my way out. By the way, you'd better get this window repaired. Police funds'll pay for it.'

When White left him, Nisbet got up to return the files to the cabinet. He automatically put them back as he had found them, white tags to the front, then the green, and finally the blue. The tags on the files were staggered. It was when he replaced the blue-tagged files that he paused – there was no doubt about it, there was a gap – one file was missing. He registered the fact but realised it might not be significant. Torvil might have taken the file home, or it might be locked up in his car.

He turned his attention next to the dead man's diary. The entries in it were of the briefest – times of appointments, initials, expenses incurred, and so on. In the Address and Phone Numbers section he found most of the names which figured on the blue tags. With quickening interest, he jotted down on a pad the names which occurred in the diary but were not represented on the blue tags in the filing cabinet. There were only four of them. They might be worth following up, he thought. One of them might be the name on the missing file.

He looked again at the diary pages, turning to the current week. Fred Briggs had seen the body through the window on March 16. Pretty certainly Torvil had shot himself the evening, or during the night, before. He certainly couldn't have done it during the daytime on the 15th, when all the offices would have been occupied and the shot would have been heard. He looked at Torvil's diary entry for the day before, March 15. It was brief: DS 8pm. He looked at the pad on which he had scribbled those names. One of the names was Derek Sillitoe.Coincidence? He wondered.

By now Nisbet was beginning to have second thoughts about the suicide. True, the body was found in a room of which the only door and both windows were locked. True, also, that the revolver was found in the dead man's hand. The forensic people would soon be reporting on the revolver and on any fingerprints found on it. Meanwhile Nisbet decided he would keep an open mind about the suicide. He recalled now that when he had first heard, and then read, the Constable's report, he had been vaguely troubled about that loose key found on the floor beside the body. Why didn't Torvil keep that key on his keyring along with the others?

An idea occurred to him and he got to his feet at once to test its feasibility. He took up the mat from the floor by the desk, rolled it up loosely, and laid it on the floor in the centre of the room, where the body had been found. Then he went out of the room onto the landing, closing the door behind him. Bending down, he laid the key on the floor at the foot of the door and gave it a smart kick with his foot. Entering the room again, he was delighted to see that the key had come to rest against the rolled-up mat. The 'suicide' was indeed beginning to look like murder. He thought again of the missing file. Whoever had taken it was likely to be the man he was after. And that man might very likely be Derek Sillitoe.

He made some discreet enquiries, and learned that Derek Sillitoe worked for Milton Keynes Avionics. Nisbet wasn't too sure what avionics were, but his dictionary told him that the word meant 'the science and technology of electronics applied to aeronautics'. Just the sort of new Hi-tech industry they like in Milton Keynes, he thought.

On the phone, explaining that he was a Police Officer, he asked if he could meet the Managing Director. 'Not at your place,' he added, 'but somewhere private'. Surprised but intrigued, the Managing Director agreed, and suggested the White Hart in Buckingham as a suitable venue.

'What on earth is this all about?' asked Templeton, as they settled with their drinks in a secluded corner of the Lounge Bar.

'I'll come to that in a moment,' said Nisbet, 'but first tell me something about MK Avionics. Would I be right in thinking that the work you do is hush-hush?'

'Well yes, some of it is. It's government work, for the Ministry of Defence and so on. Why?'

For answer Nisbet reached into his pocket and brought out his Police Warrant. 'Should have shown you this to begin with,' he said. 'Sorry about that. I'm not asking out of idle curiosity I assure you.'

Templeton said: 'You were asking about security. Well, there are two reasons why we have to be careful. The first is because some of our work is for the Ministry of Defence. But on top of that we have to worry about industrial sabotage as well. Our competitors sometimes get too interested in what we are doing.'

'And have you had any cause to worry about this recently?'

'Well yes, we have. One or two odd things have happened in the past year – drawings missing, parts disappearing and so on. Nothing too serious yet, but we were beginning to worry. As a matter of fact we put the matter into the hands of an Inquiry Agent. We're expecting his report any day now.'

'Would that be James Torvil?'

'Yes. How did you know that?'

'James Torvil is dead. It looked like suicide, but I think it was murder.'

'Good God! Was he murdered because of the work he was doing for us?'

'Who knows. When you called him in, did you have a particular suspect in mind?'

'No, nobody in particular. There's been nothing to point to any one individual.'

'How about Derek Sillitoe?'

Templeton looked astonished. 'You must be joking!' he said. 'It couldn't possibly be Derek. He's far and away the best man we've got.'

'Tell me about him. Where does he come from? He's English I suppose?'

'Of course he's English. And he's brilliant. He trained in America, MIT as a matter of fact.'

'MIT?'

'Massachusetts Institute of Technology – its *the* place in our field.'

'And do you work for any other Government – besides our own, I mean?'

'Sometimes. We're doing something now for the Australian Government, and, not long ago we did something for the Norwegians. A few years back we did a lot for South Africa, but that's all stopped now – it's ruled out by the military sanctions.'

When they parted, Nisbet told Templeton to say and do nothing to alert Sillitoe. 'As I've told you,' he said, 'there may be nothing in it. It's simply that Sillitoe's name and address were in Torvil's diary, and the initials DS are written in the diary for the day he died.'

Two days later, after following up other matters, Nisbet called to see Sillitoe. If Sillitoe was surprised by the visit, he gave no sign of it.

'What do you know about James Torvil?' asked the detective.

'Never heard of him. Who's James Torvil?'

'Where were you on the night of March 15?'

Sillitoe took out his diary and consulted it. 'Ah yes, I was at the Latimer Theatre, went to Jack Bannister's new play. I'm a fan of his and never miss his shows.'

Sillitoe was just a touch too voluble, thought Nisbet. 'What sort of play is it then?'

In reply Sillitoe gave him a quick thumbnail sketch of the plot. And then, for good measure, Sillitoe said: 'Well I'm blowed! I've still got the ticket stub – look.'

And that was Sillitoe's first mistake, because the painstaking Nisbet, making a routine check-up call next day at the Latimer Theatre, learned that on the night in question Jack Bannister had been taken ill at the end of Act I, and his understudy took over for the remainder of the play. Strange that his ardent fan hadn't mentioned that!

Nisbet spent some time after this in consultation with MI5 and with the Immigration authorities. He also had another long private session with Templeton. They discussed the work MK Avionics had done for South Africa in the past, before such dealings became illegal. Templeton agreed that South Africa might well be interested in their current work, and that it was more than likely that knowledge of their latest developments would be of considerable assistance to South Africa.

This was all very well, but there was still no evidence either to connect Sillitoe with South Africa, or to incriminate him for Torvil's murder. Nisbet had taken to going back to Torvil's office whenever he could. He would sit at the dead man's desk, almost willing himself to see what had happened there that night. As he was sitting there one day the phone rang. He picked it up and a voice asked: 'Are you James Torvil, and will you take a reversed-charge call from Johannesburg?' On instinct Nisbet said yes, and seized a pencil. The caller in South Africa came on the line and said:'I've checked out what you asked me; the answer is yes, the South African Security people do have a man planted in MK Avionics. He goes by the name of Derek Sillitoe, but his real name is Dirk du Toit.'

'Thank you very much!' said the delighted Nisbet, and hung up.

He called on Sillitoe again next day. 'Tell me again about the Bannister play,' he began. Sillitoe frowned, and then repeated much of what he had said on the previous visit.

'Fine,' said Nisbet, 'only trouble is, Jack Bannister was taken ill that night and couldn't finish the play – his understudy had to go on. Funny you didn't notice that, you being such a Bannister fan.'

But Sillitoe didn't bat an eyelid – he was clearly able to think on his feet. 'Ah!' he said, 'that's awkward. Fact is, I wasn't at the theatre that night. I was in Brighton for the night with a colleague's wife, so you can see why I had to cover up.'

Nisbet held up a hand. 'Let's save us both some time,' he said. 'Let me tell you where you really were that night, and what you were doing. About 8 o'clock that night you went to Albion House. You went up to Room 24 on the second floor. You found Torvil there, and you shot him in the right temple at about two feet range. You wiped the gun clean of prints and put it into Torvil's hand. You pulled his keyring from his pocket, took the key of the office door off the ring and put the keyring back in his pocket. Then you let yourself out, taking with you Torvil's file on you. You turned off the lights. When you'd locked the door from the outside, you slid the key under the door hoping it would end up somewhere near the body.'

Nisbet paused, and then said: 'Does that sound fairly

accurate to you, Dirk du Toit?'

It was hearing his real name which froze the self-styled Derek Sillitoe. It only remained for Detective Inspector Nisbet to say, formally: 'Dirk du Toit, I arrest you for the murder of James Torvil on March 15 of this year. Anything you say . . .'

FOUR

Clerical Error

That winter, in the year of our Lord 1192, was the coldest anybody could remember. Crouched over his desk in the Scriptorium at Bradwell Abbey, Brother Lawrence almost cried with pain as he put down his quill pen. He slapped his arms round his chest in the hopeless attempt to bring circulation back to his hands and arms. He looked round the room in the fitful light of the oil lamp, and looked down again at the work on his desk. And he sighed – so many hours he had already spent on this task – and so much remained to be done. Raising his chapped hands to rub his chillblained ears, he steeled himself to resume his work.

At five o'clock on this bitter winter's day it was absurd that Brother Lawrence should still be working in so poor a light. The strain on his eyes was almost as trying as the numbness induced by the cold. But the Abbot – he who must be obeyed – was insistent. The work must go on till the task was completed. The Manorial Rolls on which he was labouring must be completely transcribed, and they must be finished by the day after tomorrow.

Why this was so it was not for Brother Lawrence to question. If Father Abbot said it must be done in that time, then in that time it must be done. So Brother Lawrence bent to his task again, and the work of transcribing the folios in Norman-French went on.

Meanwhile, elsewhere in the Abbey, the Abbot was preparing to receive a visitor. The visitor, when he came, was clearly reluctant to be seen by any of the brethren. With his cape wrapped closely round him and with its hood obscuring his face, he hurried through a side gate, tapped on the door of

It was a bitter winter in 1192 at Bradwell Abbey.

the Abbot's office, and was admitted.

'Here, Father Abbot, are the last four folios to be transcribed.'

The visitor extracted the rolled folios from his sleeve and held them out. The Abbot exploded with anger. 'Not more!' he shouted, 'you said you had already brought the last ones on Tuesday. It will be impossible for Brother Lawrence to finish these as well as all the others by tomorrow night.'

'Then put some of the other Brothers on to help him.'

'Certainly not,' said the Abbot. 'It is already dangerous enough to involve Brother Lawrence in this. It would be folly to involve others. It cannot be done.'

'May I remind you,' said his visitor, 'that my Lord, Hamon le Breton, *demands* that it be done. You, as Abbot, must surely realise the consequences to the Abbey if it is *not* done.'

The Abbot understood the threat behind those words. With ill-grace he accepted the four folios, and his visitor left the Abbey as furtively as he had arrived.

Making his way in the darkness the Abbot went over to the Scriptorium. Brother Lawrence looked up at his entrance and winced as he saw the extra folios in the Abbot's hand.

'My son,' said the Abbot, 'bear with me. I know how tired you are. I can only ask you to press on with this task until it be done. The future of

Father Abbot went over again to the Scriptorium.

our Abbey is in your hands. May the Lord give you courage and strength to persevere.' And Brother Lawrence wearily crossed himself as the Abbot raised his hand in blessing.

As he returned to his own quarters the Abbot recalled the circumstances which had led to this crisis. The Abbey was caught up in the rivalries and quarrels between the Lord of the Manor of Longville and that of the Manor of Wolverton. In the bitter dispute between the Giffards and the Hamons, the Abbey was the hapless victim.

The dispute had gone on for many months. At stake were rich lands and the power that went with them. He recalled how many weeks ago an emissary from the Lord of the Manor of Wolverton had visited him secretly. It was then that the Abbot had been asked to falsify the Manorial Rolls. He had been told all too clearly what would happen to him and to his Abbey is he refused to comply.

So the whole sorry saga had begun. And now, in less than two days' time, the matter would be resolved one way or the other. For in two days' time the quarrel between the Lords of Longville and of Wolverton would be judged by no less a person than the Papal Nuncio himself sitting in Oxford.

The falsifying of the Manorial Rolls had been done subtly and judiciously. Care had been taken not to be too blatant. 'Mustn't over-egg the pudding' was the phrase used by the emissary of the Lord of the Manor of Wolverton. So the changes in the transcriptions had been minimal, but crucial none the less. In the Norman-French folios key words were changed – not too many of them, but enough to give Wolverton the edge over Longville. For instance, the 'x' in the word prix, meaning cost, was replaced by the letters 'se', changing prix into prise, cost into taking. And so on, in perhaps a score of key words in the documents.

Working through the night, the exhausted Brother Lawrence completed his task at last. By the afternoon of the following day he handed to his Abbot the final folios, and then he collapsed. Some of his brethren, mystified by all the strange goings-on, carried him to the Abbey's Infirmary.

Two days later in Oxford the Papal Nuncio sat in judgement. Present in court before him were the Giffards and the Hamons, Lords of the manors of Longville and Wolverton, each with their courtiers. The Abbot of Bradwell was there too, nervously telling his beads as he sat at the back, hoping to be unnoticed. Ecclesiastical lawyers were there in full fig, and the cut and thrust of debate filled the hours.

Slowly but surely the case for the Lord of the Manor of Longville began to prevail. On the great oak table in the middle of the courtroom were spread the manorial rolls on which poor Lawrence had laboured so long.

There came a moment when the Papal Nuncio demanded to be told by whose hand these Norman-French documents had been written. Reluctantly the Abbot of Bradwell told the Court that the documents had been transcribed by Brother Lawrence. It was at this point that the lawyer for the Lord of the Manor of Longville sprang his trap. Like a magician producing a rabbit from a hat, he tabled for the Court's inspection other copies of the manorial rolls. He invited the court to compare these with the folios lying on the great oak table. With great skill he drew attention to the few but vital discrepancies between the two sets of documents.

The Papal Nuncio sternly demanded an explanation from the Abbot of Bradwell. The poor Abbot could only stammer and say that perhaps Brother Lawrence's transcriptions contained a few clerical errors.

The Papal Nuncio, who was nobody's fool, rose to his feet. 'Father Abbot,' he said, 'this is indeed a matter of clerical error, but the clerical error is yours. And for the deceit that you have practised I hereby deprive you of your Abbey. Repent your error while you have time, and be gone, unworthy cleric that you are.'

Brother Lawrence never did know why his Abbot didn't return from Oxford, and in due time he learned to give his unquestioning obedience to a new Abbot of Bradwell.

FIVE

Jammy Strikes Again

CID officers of the Thames Valley Police were in conference at the Oxford HQ. Each of the six men present had been given a photostat of the scrawled message. It comprised only four lines, as follows:

COLLECT A VIA LEEDS
CASTLE BROM
SOUTH MAN 1912
DROP LAKES 14

This scrawled message had been discovered in the course of an investigation into drug-running. It was thought to be important, but so far had been too cryptic to be of much help. Going round the table, the Super asked each of his officers to say what he made of the scrawl.

Chalky White concentrated on the geography of it. 'Seems pretty obvious,' he said, 'that whatever is collected at Leeds goes on to Castle Bromwich and South Manchester, and possibly ends up in the Lake District.' Six pairs of eyes switched to the map on the wall and followed the route thus described.

Dusty Miller said, diffidently, 'Perhaps "A" is a person, not a thing. In other words, COLLECT ADAMS, or ATKINS, or whoever at LEEDS.' He paused, and then went on: 'But it doesn't say AT Leeds, it says VIA Leeds. Odd, that. How do

34

you collect someone or something VIA somewhere?'

Lofty Prescott, when his turn came, concentrated on line 3. SOUTH MAN 1912. 'That 1912, he said, 'could be a map reference, on a street map, say, of South Manchester. Or it could be a date, the 19th of December. Or it could be a time – twelve minutes past seven, 7.12pm in other words.'

Tiny Rawlings said: 'I reckon we should concentrate on the verbs. There are only two of them – COLLECT and DROP. Seems obvious to me that whatever is collected at Leeds is going to be dropped at Lakes. So Lakes either means the Lake District, as Dusty said, or Lake is a person, in which case Lakes on the paper ought to have an apostrophe. In other words whatever is collected is going to be delivered at LAKE's place. 'Whoever Lake is,' he added.

Apart from the Super himself, only one man remained to add his contribution, and that was Jammy Barker. He already had the nickname of Jammy when he had been transferred to Oxford from Milton Keynes CID. The name arose from what his colleagues thought was his phenomenal luck in clearing up cases. Jammy himself took this in good part, but preferred to think it was more a matter of logic and commonsense than good luck. With a nickname like Jammy, and a surname like Barker, it wasn't surprising, perhaps, that his surname was sometimes changed in a way that seemed to reflect on his parentage. Jammy wasn't too happy about that.

While the others had been speaking, Jammy had been scribbling. He picked up the pad on which he had been writing. 'We've all been taking these four lines one by one,' he said, 'but perhaps they should all be read as one line.' He read out what he had scribbled down:

COLLECT A VIA LEEDS CASTLE BROM SOUTH MAN 1912 DROP LAKES 14

'How does that help?' asked the Super.

'Well,' said Jammy, 'Leeds Castle is down in Kent. And so is Bromley South.'

'Then what about MAN 1912?', said Dusty Miller.

'I reckon,' said Jammy, 'that if we look in the Railway Timetable, we'll probably find an Intercity train leaves Bromley South at 1912 for Manchester.'

'That's easily checked,' said the Super, and reached for the phone. In a matter of minutes British Rail confirmed the fact, and added that Bromley South is where the local service from Bearsted, nearest station to Leeds Castle, would join the Intercity Service.

'I've been there,' said Lofty Prescott. 'It's a real tourist attraction.' JH

'It all fits so far,' said the Super, 'but what about A VIA LEEDS CASTLE?'

'I've been to Leeds Castle,' said Lofty Prescott. 'It's a real tourist attraction. And apart from the castle itself, standing in the middle of a lake, there is also an Aviary. Could that be it? Should the first part read: COLLECT AVIARY LEEDS CASTLE? In other words the pick-up is to be made at the Aviary. With so many tourists milling around, that would provide plenty of cover.'

'Right,' said the Super, 'let's see what we've got. The drugs are brought to Leeds Castle, probably brought over through one of the Channel Ports. The courier meets our villain in the Aviary and hands him the parcel. Chummy then makes his way to Bromley South and catches the 1912 Intercity train to Manchester. What does our villain do next? He's obviously going to deliver the drugs to someone else. Where? and When?'

'DROP LAKES 14', said Jammy. Could that mean the 14th of the month? If so, and if it's this month, we've only got two days.'

The Super said: 'Well, we can get the Kent CID to watch the Leeds Castle meet. We'll tell them to keep observation on the 14th in the Aviary, but not to interfere with the handover. They can arrest the courier after our villain has left with the drugs, but not before. Trouble is, where will our villain be going with the drugs? Kent CID can put a tail on him and travel with him on that 1912 Intercity from Bromley South. After that we'll have to wait to see where the trail ends.'

Jammy coughed. 'Super,' he said, 'I know this will sound a bit far-fetched. But I used to live in Bletchley and the fact is that just as the railway enters Bletchley the line passes right alongside the Lakes Estate. It could just be that DROP LAKES 14 means exactly that – that our villain has got to drop the drugs off the train on the 14th as it passes the Lakes Estate. That wouldn't be too difficult. On the other side of the track, opposite the Lakes Estate, there's just open country, a rough area where there used to be brickfields. There were great ponds there, but they've been filling them up, and now it's just a derelict piece of land. It'll be nearly half past eight by then, and quite dark.'

The Super pondered this for a bit. 'Worth a try,' he said, 'we can tell Kent their man can arrest Chummy after he throws the drugs off the train. And we'll have our men posted to arrest whoever collects them.'

And that is exactly how it all came to pass. Jammy Barker had struck it lucky again.

SIX

The Big Tickle

The playground at St. Clements C of E Primary School in Milton Keynes was empty. The Lollipop Lady had shepherded the last of the children across the road and had herself gone home. In the school itself the lights were out in the classrooms. Only in the Headmaster's room was there any sign of life. There, Mr Greaves and his small staff were still on duty.

The cause of this after-school meeting, little Percy Snyder, was not present. Not present in the flesh, that is, yet in his absence he was very much there. His class teacher, Winifred Dow, explained to the Head and to her colleagues why she was so worried about him. It arose from the fact that four young children, Percy among them, had, allegedly, been caught shoplifting at the local Woolworth's.

Ten year old Percy attended St. Clements, the other three slightly older children did not. Miss Dow was convinced of Percy's innocence. That he had been in the store that Saturday morning could not be denied. 'But he told me that he was not with those other boys and didn't even know them, and I believe him. The School must take some action, otherwise a great injustice will be done.'

'What do you suggest?' asked the Head.

'Can't you speak to the Police, or to the Manager of

38

Woolworth's, or even to the Magistrate if it comes to that?' said Miss Dow.

Mr Greaves and the other three teachers heard her out with some embarrassment. She really was getting rather hysterical, they thought. Two of them, in whose classes Percy had been before he moved up to Miss Dow's, couldn't share her estimate of Master Percy Snyder's good character. In their experience Percy's air of wide-eyed innocence was always an act designed to get him out of scrapes.

Looking surreptitiously at his watch, Mr Greaves sought to close the meeting. He agreed that the good name of St. Clement's School was at risk – he conceded that if Percy *was* innocent he must be protected. And finally he agreed that he would have a word with the Police and with Mr Stuart, the Manager of Woolworth's.

Whether he ever did or not, and, if he did, whether it made any difference, Mr Greaves was not prepared afterwards to say. For the record, the Police themselves decided that they wouldn't press charges against Percy, and Mr Stuart went along with this. Mr Greaves was relieved, Miss Dow was delighted, and her two colleagues were cynical.

So Percy's scholastic career continued uninterrupted. A year later he faced the ordeal of the eleven plus exam. On its result depended his future schooling – either in a Technical School or in Secondary Education. He completed one of the two tests. While sitting for the other one he was taken ill and was led from the exam room vomiting. The Examination Board Members, who didn't know that self-induced vomiting was one of Percy's party tricks, decided that he ought not to be penalised for being ill. So he was awarded the place he wanted at the Secondary School.

His years there were not distinguished academically. He moved up the School always in the bottom third in each form. He contributed little to the school in the field of sport, showing neither enthusiasm nor skill. So the staff was surprised when he entered for the Sponsored Half-Marathon. It was to raise money for a new mini-bus for the school. Besides training for the run, entrants were expected to knock on doors throughout the neighbourhood to seek sponsors. Percy did his share of this and handed in two sheets of sponsors' names. He completed the Half-Marathon and was given back the two sheets of sponsors' names. He made the round of their houses to collect the sums each had promised. As a result Percy was able to hand in a creditable £18–50 towards the mini-bus fund. But unknown to anyone but himself he also collected a further £21–80 from the names on two other sheets of which the school authorities knew nothing – a nice little 'earner' for himself.

Fortune continued to favour him when he left school. He got a job immediately, while many of his contemporaries didn't. It wasn't a very smart job, but then his CSE results had not been very impressive either. This didn't worry his first employer – he simply wanted a bright lad to work with him on his stall at the markets. Percy fitted the bill very well and learned fast. He didn't need telling twice about any of the tricks of the trade – he grasped them at once and came up with some new ones of his own invention.

He became a little too clever. His boss caught him out in a fiddle, not against the public, but against the boss! That should have got him the sack, but Percy said, in his most disarming way, that of course if he lost his job, he would have to tell the wholesaler, from whom they got the goods for the stall, one or two things which might make the wholesaler rather angry. So he wasn't sacked and continued in his employment for another eighteen months.

By then Percy felt he was ready to set up on his own. And he prospered. Both in his trading, and in the quite considerable volume of odd jobs he undertook, he became skilled at manipulating the VAT Regulations. He was careful not to be too greedy and for a long time his VAT Returns aroused no queries. Later, he did have one brush with an Inspector. But he survived – his air of candour in admitting to a careless oversight disarmed even a cynical VAT Inspector.

So young Percy Snyder was getting on. One of his favourite sayings was: 'They can't touch you for it.' He meant by this that while looking after Number One, you must always be careful to preserve appearances. Plausibility became his long suit. He looked and sounded so *honest*. In his young adult life, just as in his schooldays at St. Clement's, he could look you in the eye, and your suspicion that he was pulling a fast one would just melt away.

Some judicious second-hand car dealing enhanced his growing bank balance. So did the series of sales he organised – of bankrupt stock and warehouse clearances. He was careful not to repeat these too often in the same town. Throughout Herts, Beds, and Bucks he did very well and was becoming positively rich!

But not rich enough, or fast enough, to please himself. What I need, he told himself, is a really big tickle. He did pull off one major coup which netted him a considerable sum. It was an insurance fraud involving loss of stock through fire. He relished the cash it brought him but vowed he wouldn't try that again. It had meant relying on a second party – the expert fire-raiser he had employed to carry out the arson. The Insurance Company withheld payment for months, and though they finally paid up, Percy was determined not to go down that road again.

He realised he had had a lucky escape and for some time would have to be very circumspect. He decided it would be no bad thing if he dropped out of sight for a while. So, now well able to afford it, he went off to South Africa for a holiday.

He had no plans and didn't know how long he would be away. 'Just until the heat's off,' he told himself, and remembering the arson, he smiled. For two weeks he stayed in a fairly unpretentious hotel in Johannesburg. Subconsciously he was appraising the country. Could it be here that he could organise the big tickle? Moving out of his hotel he rented a small apartment on a short lease.

In a bar one evening he fell into conversation with a South African, Kurt Swanepoel. They got on well together and met in the same bar on subsequent evenings. Each seemed to see in the other a kindred spirit. Kurt was from Kimberley and was only in Johannesburg on leave. He told Percy he was a Clinic Orderly in charge of the First Aid Station at a diamond mine. When his leave was finished he invited Percy to visit Kimberley. 'See a bit more of the country, man, Jo'burg isn't the only place.' Percy accepted the invitation and a few days later followed Kurt to Kimberley.

He was fascinated by all he saw and was intrigued by the high level of security everywhere. Because of his job Kurt was able to move freely about the mine, and Percy, within limits, was able to accompany him.

By now they knew each other very well and realised how much they had in common. Kurt was as natural a con-man as Percy, though he lacked Percy's experience. He listened with envy as Percy recounted some of the strokes he had pulled in England. Like Percy, Kurt too dreamed of a big tickle that would make him rich.

Inevitably their thoughts turned to diamond smuggling – not gemstones, but industrial diamonds. No industry in the world is so thoroughly organised to prevent smuggling as the diamond industry. Even so, the idea wouldn't go away. The difficulties might be great, but the pay-off would be tremendous if only they could pull it off.

When Percy left to return to Johannesburg they had not yet worked out a plan for the big tickle they both longed for. 'Leave it to me,' said Kurt, 'if I come up with anything I'll get in touch.'

Ten days later Kurt phoned Percy. He was very guarded on the phone but Percy sensed his excitement. Kurt said he would fly to join him in Jo'burg on the following Friday night. Meanwhile Percy was to book them two seats on the Sunday flight to London. The big tickle was taking shape.

Percy booked the two seats on South African Airways. He cancelled the lease of the apartment, effective from the same Sunday, agreeing to forfeit his deposit because of the short notice.

42

Meanwhile, in Kimberley Kurt had achieved the impossible. Using the freedom of movement afforded by his job he succeeded in stealing a large quantity of industrial diamonds. He did this late on Friday afternoon, confident that this would give them the weekend before the loss of the stones was discovered. From his clinic he took home all the material he would need for setting a limb in plaster. Then he caught his plane to Johannesburg.

At Percy's flat the two men gloated over the haul of industrial diamonds poured out on the table between them, and Kurt explained his plan. On the Saturday Kurt put Percy's right arm and shoulder in plaster, using all his professional skill. Into the plaster went a fortune in industrial diamonds.

At Jan Smuts Airport on the Sunday there was lots of sympathy for Percy from the airline officials at the check-in desk. They arranged for Percy and Kurt to board the aircraft ahead of the other passengers. The cabin crew also were very solicitous for Percy's comfort during the flight.

At Heathrow Percy and Kurt were invited to leave the aircraft first. In the Terminal building, too, officials went out of their way to be helpful. Outside Terminal 3 they boarded a taxi and were on their way into London.

It was as they passed Heston on the M4 that the accident happened – a crash involving a lorry and their taxi. Kurt and the taxi driver were killed outright. Percy was badly smashed up, unconscious but still alive. At the hospital the doctors knew that they must remove the plaster and reset the arm and shoulder without delay. So the unconscious Percy lost the plaster – and a fortune in industrial diamonds! He recovered consciousness three days later, to find a Police Constable sitting by his bed. The big tickle was over.

Looking to the other side of the bed, he saw a grey-haired old lady. Miss Winifred Dow, long retired now, had read about Percy's terrible accident in her paper, and wanted to be at his side to do what she could for him, just as she had done all those years before at St. Clements C of E Primary School in Milton Keynes.

SEVEN

If Only He Had Waited!

The Independent University of Glastonbury was about to appoint a new Vice-Chancellor. The choice of the right man had exercised the minds of the Senate members very greatly. As had been found at Buckingham a few years before, it is not the easiest thing in the world to launch a new, independent University, and at Glastonbury they had been grateful for the sympathetic advice they had received from Buckingham. They had succeeded against great odds at Buckingham, and the success there had encouraged those who wished to see that success repeated. So the University of Glastonbury had been founded. Much was made, in the propaganda which preceded its birth, of Glastonbury's long history. Was it not the burying place of King Arthur and his Queen Guinivere? And looking back many centuries before that, could it not be said that Glastonbury had been the very cradle of British Christianity?

The brave venture almost failed. It was reckoned by many that the anxieties and difficulties of its first three years had helped to bring about the premature death, at fifty-eight, of its first Vice-Chancellor. Now its Senate was faced with the task of finding his successor.

They had deliberated long – they had taken soundings – they had weighed up the alternative merits of choosing a populist figure against the attractions of choosing some man of great learning. They had their disappointments. Some who had been approached simply didn't want to know. Now the moment of decision was at hand. Possible candidates had been reduced to two. Each had been asked privately if he would accept were he to be chosen, and each had said yes. Both of them, as it happened, were Oxford graduates, but only one of them could be regarded as an academician. So he was reckoned by most to have the better chance of appointment.

He was Dr James Hanover, an historian, and the Librarian of Powys College in the University of Oxford. The fact that among his many books there was one which was regarded as the definitive work on the history of Glastonbury Abbey was taken to be a big plus for his candidacy. But more to the point, he was among those comparatively few scholarly people who make a name for themselves on television. His series called 'The Past is our Future' had been widely acclaimed.

But the other candidate had two things going for him: he was a black man, and he was immensely wealthy. He came from Monrovia and his name was Siaka K Penrose. His African nationality was a very real attraction. Like Buckingham, Glastonbury looked overseas for a large proportion of its students. So its image would be greatly enhanced in the eyes of the Third World Governments if it had an African Vice-Chancellor. Furthermore, his great wealth had enabled him to be a conspicuously generous benefactor to educational causes. When he came down from Oxford he had returned to Monrovia, but after some years he had come back to Britain and now lived here, pursuing his various business interests.

So there it was, a small field of two, and both runners were now in the starting-gate. The Senate would meet on Wednesday 15th to make its choice which would be announced on Friday 17th, and the Installation of the new Vice-Chancellor would take place the following week.

It has to be said that the nation was not exactly holding its breath – the country at large was either completely ignorant of, or totally indifferent to, the whole affair. But to just a tiny handful of people it was the subject of great interest and much discussion.

One of those few who took a great interest in the matter was the eccentric playboy, Nathaniel King. He was an inveterate gambler. The tabloids loved him and were always recording his bizarre bets. He had the extraordinary knack of making successful wagers on the most improbable possibilities. He had made a packet, for example, when the Cambridge boat was buckled by collision with a barge. And he did pretty well when *two* Cabinet Ministers resigned in one week over the Westlands affair.

What few people knew was that Nat King was in deep financial trouble. In a way he was the victim of his own success as a madcap, sensational gambler. To stake large sums on obscure and improbable events had become an addiction with him, and recently some of his more eccentric bets had come unstuck. Unfortunately, too, he had carried over his hobby of betting on improbabilities into his Stock Exchange dealings. In other words he had taken to investing heavily in lame-duck stocks in the hope that they would surprise everybody (except himself) by sudden spectacular resurgance. It hadn't worked out, and his fingers were badly burned.

So Nat King was desperate. He knew that unless he could soon win another spectacular bet he was about to be irretrievably ruined. He needed some issue on which to gamble a huge amount, and he reckoned he had found it in the about-to-be-decided Vice-Chancellorship of the University of Glastonbury.

He needed two things. First, to find someone who would enter into the wager with him, or, rather, against him. And second, he needed to be able to place his bet with the absolute, cast-iron certainty that he would win. At his Club he tackled the first. The Vice-Chancellorship affair was a two-horse race. So he had to find *two* individuals who would accept his bet, one favouring Hanover, the other backing Penrose. By

Monday 13th he had managed to find two such people, and arranged with them, separately, to come to the Club on Thursday 16th so that the bet could be registered in the Club Secretary's office.

Meanwhile he had been working on the other necessity – that of ensuring that he would be betting on a cast-iron certainty. For this, frankly, he was relying on a piece of downright dishonesty. He found one of the servants at the Senate House in Glastonbury who could be bribed. To earn his money the servant was to eavesdrop the crucial meeting of the Senate on Wednesday 15th and to let Nat King know the decision that evening. Once in receipt of that information all that Nat would have to do would be to phone one of the two men he had tentatively agreed to bet with, to say that he wished to cry off. That would leave the way clear for Nat to meet the remaining man in the Secretary's office on the Thursday so that the bet could be registered.

It all worked out as planned. The servant rang Nat on the Wednesday evening. The meeting of the Senate was over, he said, and the decision had been taken. 'What was the decision?' asked Nat.

'I heard the Chairman say: 'So then, Gentlemen, we are agreed that the appointment goes to the Librarian.'

So Nat phoned Blenkinsop, with whom he had made a tentative arrangement to enter into a wager in favour of Penrose, to tell him that the bet was off. Then, on the Thursday he kept his appointment with Jenkins in the Secretary's office and recorded his wager for a considerable sum in favour of Dr Hanover. Nat King slept well that night. Tomorrow the announcement of the new Vice-Chancellor would be made, and Nat could collect his winnings.

Unfortunately, though, he was in for a terrible shock. The servant's hearing was not that good. What the Chairman had actually said at the end of the Senate meeting was: 'So then, Gentlemen, we are agreed that the appointment goes to the *Liberian*'.

So, when Friday came, and Siaka K Penrose was announced as the new Vice-Chancellor, Nat King was shattered. Worse than that, he was ruined. And he shot himself.

If only he had waited! In the interval between the appointment and the solemn installation of Vice-Chancellor Siaka K Penrose, Interpol officers arrived in the United Kingdom. They brought irrefutable proof that the source of Siaka Penrose's huge wealth was a series of massive frauds against the great Firestone Corporation in Monrovia.

The members of the Senate were acutely embarrassed. But at least they didn't have to cancel the Installation of a new Vice-Chancellor. They offered the appointment to Dr Hanover, and he accepted. If only Nat King had waited!

EIGHT

Jeux Sans Frontières

In the outskirts of Lerida the young British couple parked their car and trailer outside the supermarket and entered the store. They pushed their trolly round, in no great hurry, and chose from the shelves the foodstuffs they would need for the last week of their holiday.

It was a holiday to which they had looked forward with particular pleasure, and one which they felt they had earned. They had at last fulfilled an ambition – they had acquired the house of their dreams high up on the ridge at Bow Brickhill, with magnificent views over the Vale of Aylesbury. True, they had saddled themselves with a huge mortgage, but they were young, energetic and full of confidence. The mortgage repayments would be a burden for years to come, but meanwhile they would enjoy their holiday.

Kathy and Tom Harvey had been in Spain for the past fortnight, having the sort of holiday they both enjoyed. Neither cared for crowds or hotels, or for the cossetting of package tours. They preferred instead to go at their own pace, off the beaten track, able to stop and pitch their tent wherever fancy and a suitable site offered itself. The past two weeks had gone pleasantly. They had made their way through the Spanish countryside, avoiding the towns except when, as now, they needed to restock with provisions.

Their plan for their last week was to continue their touring and camping by making their way up the Segre Valley, with its series of lakes strung out like beads on a necklace. There would be the added attraction that the valley passed through mountainous country, the Sierra del Montesech and Sierra de Boumort. They aimed, finally, to go through Viella and to cross into France between Les and Fos.

They pushed the trolly out to their car, and stowed the goods into the small trailer in which their camping gear travelled. Then they were on their way again, content to be leaving towns behind once more.

The winding road delighted them, as it first left the Segre River and then rejoined it, crossing and recrossing it as they travelled northwards. After Pobla de Segur, road and river kept each other close company all the way to Lake Guingueta. Without ever hurrying, Tom and Kathy had made good progress and they decided that they could stay put for a few days. They pitched their tent between Espot and the lake.

It was in a bar in Espot that they met Norman Hirst, the first fellow-countryman they had seen for many days. It was natural that they should spend the evening together. Conversation flowed easily and they quite enjoyed his company. He was interested that they came from Milton Keynes, about which he had heard though he had never visited it. He didn't tell them where he came from, but from his talk they took him to be a Londoner. They met with him on the following three evenings too in the same bar.

It was on the third evening that he astonished them by telling them that he was wanted by the Police in England. He didn't say why and they didn't like to ask him. They had never before, as far as they knew, been in the company of a criminal. Their reaction was a mixture of embarrassment and excitement. It occurred to them to wonder why he should have told them, and the reason soon emerged.

'The trouble is,' said Norman, 'there's this new Extradition

Treaty going through. When it's signed the Spanish can hand me over to the British Police and I'd be finished.'

'So what do you plan to do?'

'I want to get out of Spain as soon as possible and go to South America.'

'How will you do that?'

'I have to get to Marseilles. Once I get there, no problem; I can get a ship from there through contacts. It's getting into France that's my problem – and you can help me.'

Tom and Kathy were startled. It was one thing to have a real live criminal confiding in them – it gave them a feeling of guilty excitement. But to be asked actually to *help* him, that was altogether a different thing.

'Look,' said Norman, 'you're gong to France anyway, on your way home. Just give me a lift over the border, that's all. Then I'll be on my way.'

'But what happens at the border? You'll be caught and we'll be in trouble.'

'No, listen,' said Norman, 'we needn't go on the main road. I know a track over the mountain which crosses the frontier where there are no barriers. I've checked it out. That's why I've been up here in this area. It's a rough track, but your car wouldn't have any problems.'

'We can't do anything like that,' said Kathy. And Tommy added: 'We certainly can't – it's not on.'

But Norman Hirst wouldn't take no for an answer. 'I'll make it worth your while,' he said. 'I can't give you actual cash, but I'll give you a cheque on my bank account in Switzerland.'

'Forget it. You're wasting your time,' said Tom firmly.

But Norman Hirst pulled out his cheque book. He made out, and signed, a 'Pay to Bearer' cheque and pushed it over the table towards them.

'Before you finally decide,' he said, 'take a look at that. It's yours, for doing practically nothing.'

Tom and Kathy looked at the cheque and looked at each other. They were silenced by the amount filled in on the cheque, and Tom immediately thought of that huge mortgage on the Bow Brickhill house, and on what such a cheque could do to ease that burden.

'I'm still not sure,' said Tom, 'but let's discuss it.'

So the three of them talked the matter over. Norman explained the proposed route, pointing it out on a map he produced from his pocket. They worked out times and distances. Norman said he was certain they'd see no other traffic. 'But to be on the safe side,' he added, 'before we get anywhere near the border, you can pull up and hide me in your trailer until we're well across. So if we do pass any other vehicle, which we won't, it'll look as if there's only you two in the car.'

So agreement was reached. Any remaining reluctance on Tom and Kathy's part had been put to flight by the size of the sum on the cheque that lay on the table between them.

Next day they set off. Several kilometres short of the border Tom stopped the car. Norman climbed into the trailer and the camping gear and their luggage was adjusted round him. Tom stretched the canvas across the trailer top and got back into the car. Norman had been right – the track was rough and steep, but it presented no real difficulty to Tom as he drove cautiously upwards. They saw nobody, and no other traffic.

There was no way of knowing exactly when they crossed out of Spain into France. Tom kept going for several kilometres more. By now they were descending and the track led them at last to within sight of a proper road. From his study of Norman's map Tom reckoned that this was the road which would lead them eventually to Pont-de-la-Taule. He stopped the car and went to the trailer to release Norman. Pulling back the canvas he was horrified to discover that Norman was dead!

He yelled to Kathy to come and join him, needing confirmation that the man was really dead – he was so staggered and appalled that he couldn't trust his own judgement. They stared, aghast, at the body and at each other, and frantically discussed what they should do. Instinct told them to abandon the trailer and its grim contents and to get away as fast as they could.

Hastily they pulled out of the trailer their personal belongings but left their tent, groundsheets and cooking paraphanalia with the body. Then, while Kathy pulled the canvas cover into position and strapped it down, Tom unscrewed the number plate from the rear of the trailer. He unhitched the trailer from the back of the car, and together they manoevred the trailer some distance off the road. Getting into the car they drove off as fast as they could.

They had seen no-one since crossing into France and when they reached Pont-de-la-Taule they drove straight through, making for St. Girons. From there they pressed on to Toulouse, where they had to stop for petrol. After that, on through Poitiers, Nantes and Rennes to St. Malo. At St. Malo they took the ferry to Plymouth. Two days later they were back in Bow Brickhill.

Unknown to them, even before they had cleared Toulouse, Henri Boudrac had found the trailer. A small-time farmer, he didn't hesitate when he saw the abandoned trailer. In no time he had coupled it behind his own vehicle, intent on getting it home and under cover as soon as possible. So, as Kathy and Tom drove northwards towards St. Malo, Henri in his barn and behind closed doors, was excitedly unstrapping the cover of the trailer. He let out a great Gallic oath and nearly collapsed when he discovered he had stolen – a corpse!

Like Kathy and Tom before him, Henri did some furious thinking. He was sure no-one had seen him take the trailer. The faster he got rid of it and its contents the better. With Gallic cunning he decided that the little autonomous republic of Andorra would be a better place to dump the body than anywhere in French jurisdiction. So, attaching a temporary number plate to the trailer, he drove it after dark into independent Andorra, parked it by the side of the road outside Casamanya, and scuttled back into France again.

So the third party to 'find' Hirst's body was an Andorran

gendarme. The Andorran authorities were puzzled. Who was this dead man? Where did he come from? How did he get here? How did he die?

Because of the French number plate Andorra tried France first, and got no satisfaction. The French didn't want the body any more than the Andorrans did. Spain next, because a Spanish address was found on a paper in the dead man's pocket.

It was established that the corpse *had* lived in Spain, but he was British, not Spanish, so Spain didn't want the body either. So the British could have him – after all he was one of theirs. But by this time Norman Hirst's identity had been established. And while the British had definitely wanted Hirst alive, they had no particular desire for his body. So, invoking the principle of 'finders keepers', they suggested that Andorra should keep him. At this point the quadrilateral communications finally petered out, with Andorra giving Norman Hirst a funeral 'on the State'.

While all this had been going on Kathy and Tom were back in Bow Brickhill. After much anxious deliberation they decided to fly out to Zurich. There, with an outward calmness which belied their nervousness they presented their 'Pay to Bearers' draft at the Bank, and walked out with a *very* handsome sum in Swiss francs.

There isn't much more to tell. Kathy and Tom were able to buy a fine new trailer. Their new-found wealth greatly eased the burden of that huge mortgage. And they spent the next splendid summer visiting all the resorts which had been chosen for that year's 'Jeux sans frontières'.

NINE

Diddled By A Diddicoy

They were all relaxed after a good dinner, friends and neighbours who all lived in and around Newport Pagnell, and the conversation flowed this way and that. For a while there had been several separate conversations going on in the Stewarts' large lounge. But, as often happens, the separate conversations merged and imperceptibly the whole company found itself joining in one topic.

And that topic was the gypsy way of life. It had started as a chat between Norman Adams and Stewart himself. The papers and the TV programmes that week had all carried stories about the gathering of some hundreds of gypsies and travelling folk in Wiltshire. As others began to join in it was clear that opinions were divided. Mavis Turner said forthrightly 'They're all a lot of drop-outs, they're not real gypsies, gypsies are quite different. They're Romanies and they've existed for hundreds of years, not only here but all over the continent as well. And if they want to be nomads, why shouldn't they?'

'That's all very well,' said Norman, 'the fact is they don't pay rates and taxes, they steal chickens, and they spoil the countryside with their encampments.'

'And what about their children's education?' asked Margaret Austin. 'Surely it can't be right to let them wander about all

'John Bunyan was a Diddicoy'.

over the country. They should settle down in one place like the rest of us, and their kids should go to school properly.'

So the conversation flowed, much of it anecdotal, and by and large the gypsies were having rather a bad press. It was when George Wainwright used the word 'diddicoy' that the conversation took a new twist. The word was new to them all, and George was asked what it meant. 'Well,' he said, 'it can mean several things. It can mean a travelling tinker or tinsmith. We have a good example of this in our own local history. John Bunyan was a diddicoy. He travelled all over this area as a tinker, mending and selling pots and pans. He did that for years before he settled down in Bedford and became the famous preacher we all know about, and wrote *The Pilgrim's Progress.*'

'So is diddicoy just another word for gypsy?' asked Mavis.

'Yes, it can be,' said George. 'Or it can also mean a scrap metal merchant – like you, Ralph' he added. That got a laugh. Ralph was without doubt the richest man there, and his wealth came entirely from scrap metal dealing.

'So I'm a gypsy am I?' he asked.

'Well, sort of,' said George.

'Then let me tell you,' said Ralph, 'something my old grandfather told me years ago.'

Most of those present had known Ralph's old grandfather, and they listened with interest to what Ralph had to say.

'This is the true story of something that happened to my grandfather towards the end of last century. He met up with a diddicoy. This particular gypsy met my grandfather one day at Aylesbury Market. My grandfather was there to sell eggs but the diddicoy wanted to sell him a horse. He trotted the horse up and down the street to show off its paces. My grandfather kept telling him he wasn't interested – he was well satisfied with the horse he already had. But the diddicoy wouldn't be put off, and finally he said to my grandfather: "Can I trust you with £200? Hold out your hands". Then he put a bag of money into each of my grandfather's hands, and another two bags of money on my grandfather's shoulders, and a fifth bag of money on my grandfather's head. "There!" he said, "I'm trusting you with £200."

"Rubbish," said grandfather, "how do I know there's £200 there?"

So the diddicoy took one bag, opened it, and poured out forty sovereigns. "Now do you believe me," said the diddicoy, as he collected back the five bags of money. "Now it's your turn," he said, "I trusted you with £200. Will you trust me with £2?" and he held out his two hands. So grandfather took two sovereigns out of his pocket from his egg money and put a sovereign in each of the diddicoy's hands.

Leaving grandfather, the diddicoy went over to the horse he was trying to sell and started running it up and down the street again to show off its paces. Grandfather noticed that each run up and down the street was getting longer each time. Just when grandfather started to move down the street himself towards the retreating horse, he was tapped on the shoulder and told that someone wanted to speak to him in the Tap Room of the pub. You can guess the rest. Grandfather found nobody waiting for him in the Tap Room, and when he came out the diddicoy and the horse had gone – and so had grandfather's two sovereigns! He chased down the street of course but couldn't see the diddicoy. But he wouldn't give up. He went back to the White Hart, got his own horse and cart, and set off in pursuit. He didn't catch the diddicoy who had diddled him but he did meet up with other gypsies, and he saw straightaway that they had the very horse he had been asked to buy. But when grandfather told them what had happened they all swore to a man that the horse belonged to them, not to the absent diddicoy.

Grandfather knew he was beaten, so sadly he went home. But he never forgot that day in Aylesbury Market when he was robbed of £2. About eighteen months later, at Leighton Buzzard Market, he saw that very same diddicoy. He tackled him at one. "You're the man who ran off with my two sovereigns," he said.

But the diddicoy said: "Oh no, you've got it all wrong – that wasn't me, that was my brother. I remember all about it because my brother told me what he had done that day".

So, even though my grandfather knew the man was lying, and was convinced that this was indeed the diddicoy who had diddled him, there was nothing he could do. "Never trust a diddicoy" he used to say to me. "I'm giving you that advice free. It cost me two sovereigns".

"And I've never forgotten that advice," said Ralph, "and nor should you".'

And on that note the party ended. All in all, gypsies, romanies and diddicoys hadn't come out of it too well.

TEN

Those That Take To The Sword . . .

There was gloom in the Barton household in Winslow. John
Barton had been made redundant. In the chill economic climate
of these days, that didn't make him unique. He was very bitter
about his redundancy, and that didn't make him unique either.
His bitterness was compounded by a secret desperation – and
that, if not unique, was something of very personal implication.

The redundancy was easily explained – the Bletchley firm for
whom Barton worked was in dire trouble. The bitterness was
easily explained too – in John's opinion there were at least three
others who should have been made redundant before him. The
desperation arose from a circumstance known only to John
himself.

Some years before he had been made sole trustee of a fund
until his nephew should reach the age of eighteen. The boy was
already two months into his eighteenth year. Much of the trust
fund had gone, swallowed up on John's desperate efforts to
recoup losses on the Stock Exchange.

Without the redundancy, there would have been problems
enough. Now those problems were compounded. And there
was so little time left to find a solution. John Barton made
frantic calculations. His redundancy payment would help, but
only partially. His wife knew nothing of his misuse of the trust

fund, and he was determined that she never should find out. Their only daughter was due to be married later in the year and he knew that his wife would expect her to be given the sort of wedding she had been promised. It gave John a cold sweat to think of what *that* would cost. In his wife's eyes it would be a proper first call on some of the redundancy money. And, anyway, she was maddeningly confident he would soon get another job, a confidence he knew he couldn't share. And, with his job gone, and so little prospect of soon finding another, he had no hope that his bank manager would be helpful about an overdraft.

All in all then, a desperate situation calling for desperate measures. As he wrestled with his problems at his home in Winslow his bitterness increased. It focussed particularly on Peter Reed, the Company Secretary. It was Reed, he was sure, who had insisted that Barton's job should be the one to go.

He agonised over his problem and could see no way out. Shame and ruin seemed inevitable. But then he heard a piece of news that set his mind racing. He learned that Peter Reed was about to go out to Uganda on Company business. As casually as he could Barton enquired how long Reed would be there. Specifically he wanted to know when Reed would return – on what date and on what plane. He managed to get the information without raising suspicion.

It was at about this time that another man, hundreds of miles away, was having his problems too. He was El Sirte, an Arab hit-man. He had been given an assignment which so far he had failed to carry out. That assignment was to assassinate Ben Moshe. Ben Moshe, an Israeli plenipotentiary, was engaged in making the rounds of certain African capitals.

El Sirte had stalked him assiduously but had so far been quite unable to get near him. He tried and failed in Lusaka. When Ben Moshe went from the Zambian capital to Dar es Salaam El Sirte followed, but in the Tanzanian capital likewise no opportunity presented itself.

Only two other possibilities remained. Ben Moshe was due to go on, first to Nairobi, and then to Kampala in Uganda. Of these, El Sirte didn't even consider Nairobi. He had too much respect for Kenyan security. So it would have to be Kampala.

Ben Moshe was expected to stay three days in Nairobi, so El Sirte retired to Mombasa on the coast, to await the time when Ben Moshe would go on to Kampala, and El Sirte could pursue him there. So it came about that when Ben Moshe flew from Nairobi to Entebbe, El Sirte also flew there from Mombasa. The two men arrived at Entebbe Airport two hours apart. Ben Moshe was met at the airport and driven into the capital, Kampala, in a Government Mercedes. El Sirte went into the capital with less fuss, on the Airport bus.

❖ ❖ ❖

In Bletchley John Barton was also planning to fly to Uganda. He told his wife he had been advised of the possibility of a job there. In reality he was putting into effect a desperate plan. As the first step in that plan he had taken out an Insurance Policy on Peter Reed's life.

When he got to Entebbe Airport he made enquiries about hotels in Kampala. He needed one of the lesser hotels – he dare not use a major hotel and risk being seen there by Peter Reed. Going into town on the Airport bus he made his way to the hotel he had chosen.

Next day came the second part of his plan, one about which he was particularly nervous. In disguise and under a false name he went to the Airline office and booked a flight on the same plane that he knew Peter Reed would be taking back to London. Barton then went back to his modest hotel and stayed there, lest by moving about in the city he might inadvertently run into Peter and ruin everything.

❖ ❖ ❖

El Sirte's plans were *not* maturing. He was having no more success in Kampala than he had had in Lusaka or Dar es Salaam. Ben Moshe was too elusive and too well protected. El Sirte was beginning to despair of being able to eliminate Ben Moshe in Kampala too. There was a fall-back alternative plan and El Sirte prepared to use it. He took steps to discover on what plane Ben Moshe would be leaving Uganda and then booked himself on the same flight.

So now all the principals in the impending drama were in Kampala – the innocent Peter Reed looking forward to his return home – the desperate John Barton, checking and re-checking the details of his plan – Ben Moshe, satisfied that his mission had gone well, and looking forward to a forty-eight hour stop-over in London before reporting back in Tel Aviv – and El Sirte, resigned now to having to use Plan B for dealing with Ben Moshe.

The fatal day came. Two planes would take off that day from Entebbe Airport. In the morning there was the Middle East Airline plane on which travelled the hapless Peter Reed. On that plane too went John Barton's suitcase. It contained a bomb. He had checked in the suitcase in the ordinary way, but of course was nowhere on hand when the tannoy announced that passengers should now board the plane.

In the evening that same day there would be the Uganda Airways plane on which were booked the Israeli diplomat, the Arab terrorist – and John Barton.

Reed's plane blew up over the Mediterranean. News of the tragedy was given on Uganda Radio. Barton heard it in his hotel room and relief flooded through him. He could look forward to a considerable sum from the Insurance Company; the Trust Fund could be topped up again in time for his nephew's eighteenth birthday, and his daughter could have the sort of wedding she dreamed of. He packed and got ready to catch the Airport bus. It would be his second trip to the Airport that day. He had gone there in the morning in his disguise and under his assumed name to check in the lethal suitcase – an experience the like of which he hoped he would never endure again. This time, as John Barton he could go boldly.

Ben Moshe and El Sirte went from the capital out to the airport in the same manner in which they had arrived – the former in a Uganda Government Mercedes, the latter on the same Airport bus that carried John Barton.

Half an hour after take-off El Sirte hi-jacked the plane, assisted by one of the Cabin Crew whose terrorist sympathies had never been suspected. They forced the pilot to land at Benghazi. Their hope, as laid down in Plan B, was that with Ben Moshe as hostage, they could bargain for the release of Lebanese prisoners held in Israel.

The plane had been directed to a runway as far away as possible from the airport buildings. It stood there in the shimmering heat. In the main cabin the steward stood with his back to the door leading to the cockpit. He was armed with a pistol in each hand. From a belt round his waist hung two hand grenades.

Inside the cockpit El Sirte, similarly armed, stood over the two pilots and the wireless operator. He barked his orders, directing the frantic conversation between the plane and the Control Tower. The Tower was ordered to convey to Tel Aviv the ultimatum that unless the Lebanese prisoners were released, Ben Moshe's life would be forfeit.

The hours went by, with the plane's passengers locked in their misery and fear. Each had his own thoughts. For John Barton there was the added dimension to the fear he felt for his own safety – what would this latest drama do to his plans for salvaging his future and his reputation?

The resolution of the stalemate came with dramatic suddenness. Israeli Commandos parachuted in. In a few hectic minutes they had taken the plane. In all the noise and confusion El Sirte and the steward were captured and Ben Moshe was released. So too were the passengers and the aircrew. There were surprisingly few casualties. Two people were badly wounded, several others only slightly.

Only one passenger was actually killed. John Barton would never now collect the Insurance on Reed. His widow in Winslow would both mourn her husband and face the shame of explaining to their nephew what had happened to his Trust Fund.

But the bitterest irony of all was that the Managing Director said that if only he was available John Barton could have been taken on again and promoted to Company Secretary in place of the late Peter Reed. Those that take to the sword . . .

ELEVEN

The Hand Of War

The year 1642 brought gloom to the whole nation, and personal tragedy to the Verney family at Claydon. In January, following the King's failure to arrest the five members in Parliament, King and Commons were on collision course, which could only lead to civil war. And in April Dame Margaret, wife to Sir Edmund Verney, died suddenly at Claydon.

Edmund Verney was appalled at the course the King was taking, yet so great was his loyalty to the throne that he stifled his fears. He was, after all, the King's right-hand man, the Royal Knight Marshall, and Standard Bearer to His Majesty. His Majesty, therefore, must be supported and obeyed. When Dame Margaret died in April, her death shattered Sir Edmund, who never fully recovered from the blow. The nation's woes, and the loss of his wife, combined to make that summer of 1642 a time of unrelieved depression for him.

Sir Edmund was not alone in his anxieties. Jacob Rendell, his right-hand man at Claydon, his chief groom and bailiff, had his problems too. Jacob shared his master's forebodings that the King's intransigence would plunge the nation into appalling dangers. And if those dangers meant that Sir Edmund must accompany His Majesty into the unknown, so Jacob Rendell knew that he must accompany his master into those same dangers. When Lady Margaret died that Easter-time, this too affected Jacob. He respected and admired the Lady of the house, but, more than this, her death meant that Celia Venables, her Companion, would now leave Claydon. And Jacob dearly loved Celia and had hoped to make her his wife. But now Celia was to leave Claydon to return to her father's farm at Bow Brickhill. With all the commotion following the death and burial of Dame Margaret, and all the urgency of Sir Edmund's departure to be at the King's side in the north of the kingdom, there could be no question of Jacob and Celia getting married. So Celia returned to Hillside Farm at Bow Brickhill, and a reluctant Jacob accompanied a troubled Sir Edmund to the north.

Refused admittance to Hull, the King turned southwards again to Nottingham. There, on 22 August, he set up his Standard. Elsewhere Royalists and Parliamentarians tasted both success and failure. Dover and Portsmouth were lost to the King, but his nephew, the dashing Prince Rupert, routed the Roundheads at Powick Bridge near Worcester.

By the last week of October, the main Royalist Army was assembled on the high ground of Edgehill near Banbury – nearly four thousand mounted troops and over ten thousand foot soldiers, with the King in their midst. And at his side Sir Edmund Verney of Claydon, his Royal Standard Bearer. Ten miles away the Parliamentary Army was massed in strength at Kineton, under its Commander, the Earl of Essex. The two armies were numerically about equal. The Royalists had more horse, but the Parliamentary army was superior in arms and equipment. The King's position on Edgehill was wellnigh impregnable – but was a defensive position what he needed? Immune from attack he might be, but strategically what he needed was the chance to sweep down from Edgehill to rout the enemy and then to make for London with all possible speed.

The King, a conspicuous figure in a black velvet mantle, with his Star and Garter over his armour, rode along the lines of his troops. Reining in his horse he paused to address them:

'My Lords and Gentlemen here present, – if this day shine prosperously for us, we shall be happy in a glorious victory. Your King is both your cause, your quarrel, and your captain. The foe is in sight. Now show yourselves no malignant parties, but with your swords declare what courage and fidelity is within you. Come life or death, your King will bear you company, and ever keep this field, this place, and this day's service in his grateful remembrance. Your King bids you be courageous, and Heaven make you victorious.'

At three o'clock on that fateful October day the battle was joined. The Royalist Cavalry charged under Prince Rupert. In the event, this was both glorious and foolish – glorious because the charge swept aside the Parliamentary lines, but foolish because, instead of wheeling to the left, where they could have had the Roundhead reserve and centre at their mercy, they continued their headlong charge straight ahead.

Meanwhile the King was left without his mounted guard, which had been given permission to charge at the head of Rupert's cavalry. So the King was undefended except for a small number of his personal footguard. Soon the infantry were locked in combat 'at push of pike'. The Royalist left wing wavered and the Roundheads pressed home their advantage. The King's Battle Standard was now the focus of the action. Sir Edmund Verney, firmly holding the Standard, was surrounded by a throng of his enemies. They offered him his life if he surrendered the Standard, but he answered above the roar of the battle: 'My life is my own, but the Standard is mine and my Sovereign's, and I will not deliver it while I live'. To wrest the Standard from him they had to hack off the hand that held it. So the gloved right hand of the King's right-hand man was trampled underfoot, and so fell Sir Edmund Verney. The faithful Jacob, only a few yards from his side, watched in horror as his master was struck down. Then he too was overwhelmed and fell to the ground as the writhing mass of infantry surged past him.

In the dusk of the October day the King himself was nearly captured, and was saved only by the timely arrival of some of Rupert's returning cavalry. Both sides were now exhausted, and when darkness fell the fighting ceased. At daybreak next morning the Royalists still held Edgehill Ridge. The enemy, despite the arrival of reinforcements, retired northwards, leaving the King undisputed master of the field of Edgehill.

Within the week the Royalists occupied Oxford and the King made that city his capital. The Roundheads established themselves at Aylesbury, and were thus in a position to deny the King a return to London.

And what of Jacob Rendell? He had seen his master killed before his very eyes, and though the talk of all around him was of the great victory the King had gained, Jacob wanted no more part of it. He wanted only to disappear, to make his way back first to Claydon, and then to seek out his beloved Celia at Bow Brickhill.

To achieve this was no easy task. The area he had to cross was frontier country, with its possession disputed by both sides. The King's forces held Oxford, Brill, Hillesden and Stony Stratford. The Roundheads held Aylesbury and its surroundings, and also Newport Pagnell. Crossing such a region was to court the risk of death or capture. Who knew, of any village, where its sympathies lay, and who knew of any cottage or farmhouse whether its occupants were friend or foe? Truly the hand of war lay heavily on the land.

But Jacob made it safely to Claydon – the great house now a house of mourning. Even more dangerous would be the remainder of his journey to Bow Brickhill. The Earl of Essex, satisfied that he held Aylesbury with ample strength, was now preoccupied with the thought that he must secure the Watling Street. He must deny it as a possible route to London to the Royalist forces, some of whom, under Prince Rupert, were known to be in the Rugby area. To this end the Earl of Essex sent troops to Fenny Stratford and the Brickhills. Danger therefore surrounded Jacob on every side as he stealthily made his way to Bow Brickhill. He dreaded what he might find when he got there. Would Hillside Farm by occupied by the enemy, and what of Celia and her family? In the event the outcome was both good and bad. The farm was intact and its family safe, but Jacob was appalled at the size of the enemy forces gathered throughout the Brickhills. The churches of all three villages were occupied, their towers providing perfect observation posts. But one of the three rectors agreed in great secrecy to marry Jacob and Celia late one evening in the farmhouse at Bow Brickhill.

Over the next few months, exercising extreme caution, Jacob did his best to discover the strength and disposition of the Roundhead forces. Most of them were bivouacked on Brickhill Ridge. Though their numbers were frighteningly large, Jacob soon realised how ill-equipped they were, and how much in need of supplies. It was clear that their commanders feared the strength of the Royalist cavalry, and that they wanted to link up with Lord Grey's Roundhead forces in Northampton. Jacob even sensed that Roundhead morale was so low, by that summer of 1643, that some of their leaders were urging their superiors in London to open peace talks with the King.

It was borne in on Jacob that news of the poor condition of the Roundhead forces ought somehow to be conveyed to the Royalists further west on the Watling Street. Might it not be possible for Prince Rupert and his cavalry to sweep along the Watling Street and secure a mighty victory? He could turn the tide of battle for the King, and open up his way into London in triumph.

Jacob made up his mind. He himself would take intelligence of the Roundheads' condition to the Royalists. If he could only get as far, say, as Towcester, surely he could there make contact with someone who could relay the vital message further west. Celia was aghast at the risk he was proposing and at the dangers he would face. But, reluctantly, she recognised the importance of his plan.

So on a moonless night Jacob stole away. By dawn he had

safely slipped past Fenny Stratford and Slmpson. In the daylight hours he hid up in a thicket on the far side of the Woolstones. At dusk on the second day he cautiously made his way back towards the Watling Street, intending to join the road on the north side of Stony Stratford.

Just as he was congratulating himself that his plan was working, he had suddenly to throw himself into a ditch. A noisy group of men emerged from the Red Lyon alehouse. His action had been too late and he was dragged from the ditch. The men were drunk, but not so drunk that they couldn't hold him down and question him. They quickly satisfied themselves that he was a Royalist, and one of them drew a knife and cut Jacob's throat. They threw his body into the ditch and hurried away.

As Jacob's body hit the ground there fell from under his torn shirt the gauntlet of his dead master – the glove he had rescued when Sir Edmund had been slain on Edgehill Ridge on that fateful October day in 1642. Jacob had carried it as a sort of talisman ever since. Now it lay in a ditch in Stony Stratford alongside the body of the faithful Jacob. Truly the hand of war lay heavy on the land.

TWELVE

A Fence Taken

There was no other word for it but 'mania'. Railway mania gripped the country just as, earlier, Canal mania had done. For the canals' landowners, speculators and engineers had schemed and competed. Now it was the turn of yet other landowners, speculators and engineers to engage in a mad race to get rich quick. All over the country meetings were held and new Railway Companies were launched. They competed with each other, but they also competed with landowners who opposed railway construction.

Prominent in the anti-railway lobby was the Duke of Buckingham, determined to keep the railways from spreading over his land. Of the many new lines projected there was one he particularly opposed. It would have brought the detested tracks through his property at Stowe. He knew that before tracks could be laid surveys must be carried out. So he gathered his labourers and dependents together and organised them into vigilantes. They were to chase off any surveyors who turned up, and if a few heads were cracked in the process, no questions would be asked.

But the surveyors were under pressure too. The companies set up to open new lines had invested good money and they wanted a return on their investment. An Irish engineer named

Byrne was charged with the task of surveying the lands round Stowe, and he had his team of surveyors.

So the battle was joined – the Duke's posse of labourers armed with their sticks, and the engineers armed with their theodolites. Quite a few pitched battles took place as surveyors and chainmen were confronted by resolute farm labourers. Cunning was employed by both sides. For the Duke, the obvious strategy was to make it impossible for the surveyors to use their theodolites. If they couldn't be physically hounded off the land, at least they must somehow be prevented from taking their levels. So large sheets and tarpaulins were brought into play. They were erected on poles and stretched across fields and roads, denying theodolite reading.

But the engineers could be cunning too. Their strategy was twofold. First, they decided to make their survey by moonlight, figuring that labourers who had worked all day would be unlikely to be on the alert all night too. Second, the engineers divided into two teams. One team of surveyors and chainmen made a great show of activity in one area of the Duke's property, while a second team quietly went to work in another area. In that second area Byrne's men arrived with two ladders which they erected on a footpath fifty yards apart. That gave them a base-line. By taking their theodolite readings from the ladders, they achieved their levels by sighting over the top of the obstructing tarpaulins. In this way, moving the ladders laboriously from place to place they succeeded in one tiring moonlit night in surveying a crucial half mile of levels.

So one after another Railway Companies were formed and plans were made for submission to Government. In each case an Act of Parliament would be needed. Government Regulations set a date as a deadline by which the plans must be submitted.

November 30th 1847 was one such date. By midnight on that day all plans must be submitted. Throughout that day the White Hart in Aylesbury was swarming with engineers, lawyers, Parliamentary agents, and landowners or their representatives. There was a frantic last minute rush not only to get each batch of plans assembled and rolled up, but also to get them delivered to the right places by midnight. It was a complicated affair. By midnight the separate batches of plans must be handed in at places as diverse as Oxford, Reading, Hertford, Bedford and Northampton. Throughout the day post-chaises left at intervals from the yard at the White Hart in Aylesbury and sped off with the precious batches of plans.

By evening all the batches but one were on their way. The one exception was the batch of plans for the Midland Grand Junction Line which was intended to run from Northampton to Reading. Vital parts of the plan were still awaited. As the hours passed there was much clock-watching and nail biting.

It was almost eight o'clock before the Northampton plans were ready. For some time an engine with steam up had been waiting at Aylesbury Station. Attached to the engine was a single coach and the guard's brake van. At last two clerks with the precious plans rushed to the Station and boarded the train. They had fifty miles to cover to Northampton. Could they do it in time? The mad rush began.

Between Leighton Buzzard and Bletchley disaster struck – the fuel on the train was exhausted. Frantically the guard and the clerks jumped down from the train. They tore up the rails of the fence alongside the track and broke them up to fuel the engine. They managed to keep the fire in the engine going until the train reached Bletchley where more adequate supplies of fuel were available. But a vital half-hour had been lost. Could they reach Northampton by midnight? It looked doubtful.

In the event it was a quarter to twelve when they pulled up in Northampton. The two clerks leapt from the train and rushed off up the steep hill to the Office of the Clerk of the Peace on Market Square. Breathless, they banged on the door just before the clock in the nearby All Saints Church struck midnight.

But no-one answered their knock! A Policeman then appeared. He told them that the Clerk of the Peace had gone home and had left word that the plans should be delivered to his house, five minutes distance away. Desperately they rushed there, only to be told that the plans could not be accepted because it was now after twelve o'clock! Indignantly they pointed out that they had been at the Office just *before* midnight, but the official was obdurate. All through this altercation the official's front door was open, so they simply threw the plans into the house and made their way back to the station. On board the little train once more they made their way safely back to Aylesbury, arriving there at three o'clock.

Two further details complete this tale. The first is that it took a meeting of the Government's Standing Order Committee to determine whether the plans had been delivered before the deadline. Standing Committee decreed that they had been, accepting the testimony of that Policeman who had directed them to the house of the Clerk of the Peace.

The second remaining detail concerns the irate farmer whose fence had been ripped up between Leighton Buzzard and Bletchley. They listened to his complaint and tried to pacify him. 'No offence intended,' they said. 'Maybe not,' he answered, 'but a fence was taken!' It would be nice to think he was suitably recompensed – for his pun as well as for his property!

THIRTEEN

The Lamp

The 1929 collapse of the woold's banking system heralded a recession which lasted well into the thirties. Its devastating effects were felt everywhere and by everyone. The modest little firm of Faulkner & Son in Newport Pagnell was just one of the millions of businesses which collapsed. Faulkners made agricultural machinery. The firm suffered in 1931 and in 1932 it disappeared altogether.

Among its forty or so employees was Ron Taylor. When his job was lost he soon found he had little prospect of finding another. He and his wife Hilda talked the matter over anxiously. After a year on the dole, by 1933 Ron had concluded that his desperate situation called for drastic measures. He decided to emigrate. Hilda was appalled at the prospect but in the end resigned herself to it. After three trips to London to the Australian High Commission Ron and Hilda succeeded in getting Assisted Passages to Australia.

They sold their few possessions for what they could get for them and in late 1933 they landed in Sydney. Their entire resources were represented by two large suitcases and one packing case. It wasn't much with which to start a new life in a strange land. In the packing case were three items of sentimental value that neither of them had felt able to part with.

There was a stool which had originally belonged to Hilda's grandmother at Olney, and on which Hilda had so often sat as a child; there was a large carved workbox which had been a wedding present to them from Hilda's favourite uncle; and there was a brass parrafin lamp which years before Ron had saved from his parent's cottage at Hanslope when the old folk died.

For the best part of a year Ron tried to get work in Sydney. He did get a few temporary jobs, but nothing that gave them either security or prospects. In the end Ron concluded that in Sydney he would never make good. So they packed up again and tried their luck away from the big city. Ron's experience in the small firm in Newport Pagnell, making agricultural machinery, prompted him to try his luck on a large ranch up-country.

In a sense the move paid off. Ron got a secure job on a huge farm as a general handyman. The job not only gave him a wage, it also put a roof over their heads. So now they had a home of their own. In its living room the carved workbox stood on the stool, and on the box stood the lamp – a sort of corner shrine to their sentimental memories of faraway Newport Pagnell.

For some months all went well. But there were drawbacks. Hilda couldn't settle. The enormous ranch was remote, and while Ron at least had his work to give him satisfaction, for Hilda there seemed to be only loneliness, isolation and boredom. Before long their marriage began to suffer.

It was then, when he was at his most vulnerable, that Ron first noticed Melba. She was black, she was incredibly beautiful, and she was about seventeen. She lived with her Aboriginal family in a village on the very edge of the huge ranch. Ron was completely bowled over by her. Their affair began in very tentative fashion, but as the weeks went by it grew in intensity. Inevitably Hilda learned of it and she blazed with anger. Finally she turned Ron out of the house and said that for all she cared he could go and live with the Abos.

For the next few weeks Ron contrived somehow to keep up

appearances. He continued with his job, and slept in his own workshop. That his employers and his fellow workers continued unaware of the total rift between Hilda and Ron was largely due to Hilda's own fierce pride. She wouldn't forgive Ron, but neither would she let the world know of the failure of their marriage.

Ron and Melba continued their liaison, but both knew that sooner or later there would come a crisis. That crisis finally came because Ron decided to confront Melba's parents and to ask them to accept him as a husband for their daughter. Their reaction was both vocal and violent. They swore at him and chased him away with sticks and stones.

Humiliated, Ron returned to the ranch. He never saw Melba again after that and learned that her parents had sent her away. He didn't see Hilda either, except at a distance. For Ron all was desolation.

Finally he wrote a letter to Hilda. In it he begged her forgiveness. He assured her that his affair with Melba was over. He swore that nothing like this would ever happen again. Couldn't they make a fresh start? He ended the letter with a plea: 'If you forgive me, light the lamp in the window and then I'll know you want me to come home'.

But night after night there was no lamp shining at the window and Ron knew that all was lost. With no word to anyone he took advantage of a rare passing truck and left the ranch. Eventually he made his way back to Sydney.

There is a strange postscript to this sad tale. In Sydney Ron finally found work. His job was as Janitor in an office block. One of the tenants in that block was Chappell & Company, the music publishers. Ron began to pester them with songs he had written, but they turned them all down, until one day at last they accepted one of his efforts. The rest, as they say, is history. That song was an instant success and Ron made a very modest fortune from his royalties on the sheet music and record sales.

Even Hilda, upcountry, heard the song that so many were

singing, and knew its origin. The chorus of the song went like
this:

> *Pack up all my care and woe*
> *Here I go singing low*
> *Bye bye Blackbird*
> *Where somebody waits for me*
> *Sugar's sweet, so is she*
> *Bye bye Blackbird*
> *No one here can love and understand me,*
> *Oh, what hard luck stories they all hand me;*
> *Make my bed and light the light*
> *I'll arrive late tonight*
> *Blackbird bye bye.*

Did Melba, the Blackbird, ever hear the song, one wonders.

FOURTEEN

The Great Train Robbery – Mark Two

Dominic Mulenga only figures in this tale indirectly. In the late seventies he came to Britain from the Central African Republic of Liwama to study at the London School of Economics. He did well at LSE and when he returned to his own country soon found employment in Liwama's Civil Service.

He took back from Britain many happy memories of his stay here. He carried with him the diplomas he had gained in his studies. And he took back also a considerable number of books. He had delighted in the many second-hand bookshops in London and had spent many an hour browsing over the boxes of books on the pavements outside the shops. His purchases were many and varied.

His son, Wina Mulenga, was not as studious or as ambitious as his father. He was more interested in having a good time than in studying or planning for a steady career. But he enjoyed reading and read many of the second-hand books his father had brought back from Britain.

One of these books intrigued him more than all the rest. It was a volume describing the Great Train Robbery of 1963. So the young Liwaman, who had never been to Britain, read all about Linslade and Cheddington, Bridego Bridge and Leatherslade Farm. As he read about the exploits of Ronald

Wina Mulenga, in Africa, read all about Bridego Bridge. NK

Biggs, Buster Wilson, and the other villains, a powerful idea seized hold of him. He too would stage a Great Train Robbery!

In the following months he made his plans. In his own way he followed in the footsteps of those 1963 villains in Britain. Like them, he did his research thoroughly. As they did, so he too reconnoitred the ground. And, like them, he knew that his Great Train Robbery would need a large gang of participants and several vehicles.

There would be other parallels too. The Great Train Robbery in Britain in 1963 was carried out in the small hours. Wina Mulenga's robbery would also happen during the night. In both cases too, thought had to be given to choosing the right place for the robbery – somewhere remote from towns, villages, or even isolated dwellings.

There was one difference, though, between the two train robberies. The British version in 1963 turned for its success on the ability actually to halt the train in its tracks. But Wina

81

Mulenga didn't want to halt the train which was his intended victim. In fact it was essential that the train should keep going while the robbery was in progress. No, he didn't want to *stop* the train, but he did want to slow it down. But more of that later.

Great train robberies in the past were usually attempted to steal cash in large quantities – either bullion or, as in the case of the 1963 robbery in North Bucks, millions of pounds worth in used bank notes. Wina Mulenga's plan was not aimed at either gold or bank notes. All the same, he expected to be appreciably richer as a result of it. And, if you want to be fanciful, you could say that the loot Wina Mulenga was after, while not actually gold, was by a coincidence golden in colour.

So where and when and how did Wina Mulenga's Great Train Robbery take place? As the *where*, the answer is, in the Central African Republic of Liwama. At to the *when*, it was in 1993. So now the rest of this brief account can concentrate on the *how*.

The background to the whole episode is provided by the disastrous drought which afflicted Central Africa in 1991 and 1992. Crops failed almost totally and starvation was widespread. Only a huge importation of maize from overseas could save the populace. And it was the transporting of thousands of tons of Yellow Maize that offered the 'gold' that Wina Mulenga was after.

The Liwama State Railway runs up the whole length of the country from south to north like a backbone. North of the Zambezi it runs for hundreds of miles, and for much of that distance through virtually empty country. In the Southern Province one long stretch of the railway offered Wina Mulenga exactly what he needed. After leaving Kolama the railway crosses a long stretch of country where there are no towns or villages at all. To right and to left there are miles of just empty bush.

In that area for a crucial stretch of about five miles the railway has to contend with a quite stiff gradient. Heavily laden freight trains have trouble enough overcoming this stiff

The lorries and trucks were hidden in the bush. JH

gradient. Wina Mulenga's simple plan was to add to the engine driver's difficulties. He would grease the rails!

He assembled his gang. He had accumulated enough old oil and grease to do the job. He put his gang to work greasing the railway lines where the gradient began. Earlier still he had recruited partners with lorries and trucks. These had arrived in the area unobtrusively over a period of days and were now hidden in the bush.

Wina Mulenga had worked out exactly how long he would need to get the rails greased. He could rely on the infrequency of trains at night, and he knew at what time he could expect the freight train carrying its precious loads of yellow maize.

At the expected time they heard the freight train approaching through the night. When it reached the rising gradient its wheels began to slip. The train slowed almost to walking pace. The troubled engine driver in his cab wrestled with his unexpected problems. He didn't see the swarms of robbers come out of the bush in the darkness. They clambered aboard the trucks, for all the world like pirates storming a hapless merchantship. Working at breakneck speed they manhandled the sacks of maize and threw them over the sides of the goods wagons. Other men at trackside gathered up the sacks and threw them into the lorries.

Up front, the worried engine driver was doing his best to coax his engine to greater effort. He had absolutely no idea of the pillaging that was going on behind him in the darkness. When at last the freight train breasted the gradient, emerging from the stretch of line that had been greased, the engine picked up speed again. Much relieved, the driver took his freight train on through the night. He was quite oblivious of the loss of hundreds of sacks of precious maize that were even now being driven away in the lorries through the bush. Eventually they found their way over the borders into neighbouring countries. There the drought and hunger had created a black market, ensuring to Wina Mulenga and his accomplices a handsome profit.

So the Great Train Robbery in Liwama in 1993 was over. Perhaps in design and scope it was less sophisticated than that other Great Train Robbery exactly thirty years earlier at Cheddington. But at least none of its perpetrators have been caught – not so far anyway.

FIFTEEN

The Turn Of The Century

The argument grew fierce in the bar of the Rose and Crown. The same argument was being waged in countless other places all over the world in that autumn of 1899.

At issue was the question: When would the 19th century end and the 20th century begin? It seemed so obvious to some that January 1st 1900 must be the first day of the new century. 'Rubbish!', said others, 'the 19th century won't end till December 31st 1900, so the new century won't begin till January 1st 1901'.

The argument grew fierce and voices grew louder and louder. Most of those taking part were more than a little drunk, so logic and commonsense were at a disadvantage.

The two sides of the argument each had a leader. On the one side was George Bunce. He was a logical sort of chap, and he insisted loudly and truculently: 'Any fool can see that this New Year's Day 1900 won't be the beginning of a new century – that won't come till the following year, January 1st 1901'.

Leading the other side was Joe Turner, an obstinate short-tempered individual. 'Stands to reason,' shouted Joe, 'December 31st 1899 must be the end of the century, so the next day, January 1st 1900 must be the beginning of the 20th century.'

So the argument went on, everybody speaking at once with more loud talking being done than listening. Gradually, though, the logical George Bunce began to prevail and finally Joe Turner stood alone, defeated. And he didn't like it one little bit. It wasn't only that he had lost the argument – it was the way the others mocked him, even those who had earlier been on his side of the argument. In a temper he stormed out of the bar, muttering to himself: 'I'll do you for this, George Bunce!'

That New Year's Eve the villagers gathered as usual at The Rose and Crown. And, as always, there was a Service at midnight in the village church. Joe Turner was absent from both, still sulking. His anger was fuelled by the way people pulled his leg. 'Have you started to celebrate the New Century?' they asked him, 'or will you wait with the rest of us till next year?'

As the new year of 1900 progressed you might have expected that the great argument would have been forgotten. But it wasn't – it smouldered on, a personal feud between the two protagonists, the logical, sensible George Bunce, and the morose and obstinate Joe Turner. This wouldn't have mattered, except that in a small village such ill-feeling between two men made everybody feel uncomfortable.

To make matters worse, a whole series of incidents occurred which first puzzled, and then annoyed, everybody. The feud not only affected the small village. News of it spread to other villages too – Tingewick, Gawcott, Twyford, Steeple Claydon, Fringford. And some of these even found themselves caught up in the affair. Twyford, for example. Twyford had an ancient tradition for the holding of an annual feast on Ascension Day. It was looked forward to eagerly and much enjoyed. People got up at four in the morning and started decorating the front of the school with boughs cut from trees. Later, dinner would be enjoyed there. By eleven everybody assembled and marched to the Church headed by the village band. After the service, everybody marched back to the school to enjoy the dinner and the rest of the day's celebration. The feast attracted folk from surrounding villages too. But on Ascension Day 1900 the happy occasion was marred by the presence of George Bunce and Joe Turner among the visitors. They quarreled, loudly and publicly and upset everybody. The shameful quarrel ended with Joe Turner shouting out to George Bunce: 'I'll meet you at Godington Feast!'

Everybody knew what that threat portended. Godington was a tiny village, too small to have a Pub of its own. It too had an ancient feast, held annually on Trinity Sunday. By long-standing custom, the village having no Pub, one of the cottages got a licence just for the week. Its owner decorated the front of his cottage with boughs and for that reason it was called The Bough House. The cottager would already have fetched a cart-load of ale and heavy drinking would follow for as long as the ale lasted.

Godington Feast was altogether a less decorous affair than the one at Twyford. What drew many visitors to Godington Feast was not only the ale. It was also the fighting which took place. Men from villages all around would go there to try their hand. Challenges that had been made months before would be settled on Godington Green. And it was all bare-fist stuff. So when Joe Turner had shouted to George Bunce: 'I'll meet you at Godington Feast!' everybody knew what it meant! Sure enough, the two men met and fought. It was a vicious affair, shameful to watch, and extremely painful to both men.

The weeks and months passed by and the feud continued. In their own village Bunce and Turner both seized every chance to score off each other. Often the incidents were petty enough. Bunce, for example, was furious when the huge pumpkin he had grown for the Annual Fruit and Vegetable Show was sabotaged. He couldn't prove Turner was responsible but he had no doubt at all it was Turner's work.

It was much the same on Guy Fawkes Night. Turner had worked long and hard to create a huge bonfire. It would be the centrepiece of the celebration on November 5th. But somebody set fire to the bonfire during the night of November 3rd. Joe knew it was Bunce – but he couldn't prove it.

By now everybody else in the village was tired of the stupid vendetta and wanted it to stop. It was ruining the usual community spirit of the village. A solution must be found.

And a solution was found – in way nobody expected. It all happened on Advent Sunday. That day by ancient tradition was known in the village as 'Milk-a-Punch Sunday'. This quaintly-named custom was just one of the hundreds of festivals which can be found all over the country. Olney has its Pancake Day; eggs are rolled down Dunstable Downs on Good Friday; Leighton Buzzard has its Simnel Cake, and so on. Well, Godington had its 'Milk-a-Punch Sunday'.

It was a simple, unsophisticated affair. Tradition said that on that day it was permissable to milk anyone's cow, and take an egg from under anyone's hen to make up a Rum Punch. What happened on Milk-a-Punch Sunday in 1900 was that very early in the morning Joan Bunce was walking along a path leading from the Turner's home. She was carrying a bowl of milk she had just taken from Joe Turner's cow. Joan Bunce came face to face with Lily Turner. And Lily had in her hand a large brown egg she had just taken from under one of George Bunce's hens.

For a moment the two women stood on the path, staring at each other. Then they both burst out laughing. Both women were utterly fed-up with the stupid feud their husbands had carried on for so long, but they hadn't known how to stop it. Minutes later Joan Bunce and Lily Turner had made their way to the Bunce cottage. Bunce, fortunately, was away that day in Buckingham and wouldn't be back until later. So the two women were able to discuss the whole ridiculous saga of the quarrel between their husbands. It was time, they agreed, to bring their husbands to their senses. But how?

They found a solution, little realising that the plan they agreed on had its origins in classical Greek mythology. Not to put too fine a point on it, both agreed to deny their husbands the marriage bed till they agreed to call off their silly quarrel.

As in the ancient Greek tale, it worked! Peace was restored and the quarrel between Joe Turner and George Bunce was well and truly over. So, as the year 1900 moved towards its end, plans began to be made for the celebration of New Year's Eve, a very special celebration this year because December 31st 1900 really would mark the end of the 19th century, and January 1st 1901 really would mark the beginning of a brand new century.

So that night, at the Rose and Crown George Bunce and his Joan, and Joe Turner and his Lily made as friendly a quartet as you could wish as they raised their glasses to toast the 20th century.

Books Published by
THE BOOK CASTLE

**COUNTRYSIDE CYCLING IN BEDFORDSHIRE,
BUCKINGHAMSHIRE AND HERTFORDSHIRE:** Mick Payne.
Twenty rides on- and off-road for all the family.   1 871199 92 1

PUB WALKS FROM COUNTRY STATIONS:
Bedfordshire and Hertfordshire: Clive Higgs.Fourteen circular country
rambles, each starting and finishing at a railway station and incorporating
a pub-stop at a mid-way point.   1 871199 53 0

PUB WALKS FROM COUNTRY STATIONS:
Buckinghamshire and Oxfordshire: Clive Higgs.
Circular rambles incorporating pub-stops.   1 871199 73 5

LOCAL WALKS: North and Mid Bedfordshire: Vaughan Basham.
Twenty-five thematic circular walks.   1 871199 48 4

FAMILY WALKS: Chilterns South: Nick Moon.
Thirty 3 to 5 mile circular walks.   1 871199 38 7

FAMILY WALKS: Chilterns North: Nick Moon.
Thirty shorter circular walks.   1 871199 68 9

CHILTERN WALKS: Hertfordshire, Bedfordshire and
North Buckinghamshire: Nick Moon.   1 871199 13 1
CHILTERN WALKS: Buckinghamshire: Nick Moon.   1 871199 43 3
CHILTERN WALKS: Oxfordshire and
West Buckinghamshire: Nick Moon.   1 871199 08 5
A trilogy of circular walks, in association with the Chiltern Society.
Each volume contains 30 circular walks.

OXFORDSHIRE WALKS: Oxford, the Cotswolds and the
Cherwell Valley: Nick Moon.   1 871199 78 6
OXFORDSHIRE WALKS: Oxford, the Downs and
the Thames Valley: Nick Moon.   1 871199 32 8
Two volumes that complement Chiltern Walks: Oxfordshire and
complete coverage of the county, in association with the Oxford
Fieldpaths Society. Thirty circular walks in each.

JOURNEYS INTO BEDFORDSHIRE: Anthony Mackay.
Foreword by The Marquess of Tavistock, Woburn Abbey. A lavish book of
over 150 evocative ink drawings.   1 871199 17 4

JOURNEYS INTO BUCKINGHAMSHIRE: Anthony Mackay
Superb line drawings plus background text: large format landscape gift
book.   1 871199 14 X

BUCKINGHAMSHIRE MURDERS: Len Woodley
Nearly two centuries of nasty crimes.   1 871199 93 X

**HISTORIC FIGURES IN THE BUCKINGHAMSHIRE
LANDSCAPE:** John Houghton.
Major personalities and events that have shaped the county's past,
including a special section on Bletchley Park.   1 871199 63 8

TWICE UPON A TIME: John Houghton.   1 871199 09 3
Short stories loosely based on fact, set in the North Bucks area.

**MANORS and MAYHEM, PAUPERS and PARSONS: Tales from Four
Shires: Beds., Bucks., Herts., and Northants.:** John Houghton
Little-known historical snippets and stories.   1 871199 18 2

**MYTHS and WITCHES, PEOPLE and POLITICS: Tales from Four
Shires: Bucks., Beds., Herts., and Northants.:** John Houghton.
Anthology of strange, but true historical events.   1 871199 82 4

**FOLK: Characters and Events in the History of Bedfordshire and
Northamptonshire:** Vivienne Evans.
Anthology about people of yesteryear – arranged alphabetically by village
or town.   1 871199 25 5

JOHN BUNYAN: His Life and Times: Vivienne Evans.
Highly-praised and readable account.   1 871199 87 5

THE RAILWAY AGE IN BEDFORDSHIRE: Fred Cockman.
Classic, illustrated account of early railway history.   1 871199 22 0

**GLEANINGS REVISITED: Nostalgic Thoughts of a Bedfordshire
Farmer's Boy:** E W O'Dell.   1 871199 77 8
His own sketches and early photographs adorn this lively account of rural
Bedfordshire in days gone by.

FARM OF MY CHILDHOOD, 1925–1947: Mary Roberts.
An almost vanished lifestyle on a remote farm near Flitwick.   1 871199 50 6

BEDFORDSHIRE'S YESTERYEARS Vol 2: The Rural Scene:
Brenda Fraser-Newstead.   1 871199 47 6
Vivid first-hand accounts of country life two or three generations ago.

**BEDFORDSHIRE'S YESTERYEARS Vol 3: Craftsmen and
Tradespeople:** Brenda Fraser-Newstead.
Fascinating recollections over several generations practising many
vanishing crafts and trades.   1 871199 03 4

BEDFORDSHIRE'S YESTERYEARS Vol 4:
War Times and Civil Matters: Brenda Fraser-Newstead.
Two World Wars, plus transport, law and order, etc.   1 871199 23 9

DUNNO'S ORIGINALS: Facsimile of 1821–2:
Little-known part of Dunstable's heritage. Anthology of prose, poetry,
legend. New introduction by John Lunn.   1 871199 19 0

DUNSTABLE IN TRANSITION: 1550–1700:
Vivienne Evans.   1 871199 98 0
Wealth of original material as the town evolves without the Priory.

DUNSTABLE WITH THE PRIORY: 1100–1550: Vivienne Evans.
Dramatic growth of Henry I's important new town around a major
crossroads.   1 871199 56 5

DUNSTABLE DECADE: THE EIGHTIES:
A Collection of Photographs:
Pat Lovering.   1 871199 35 2
A souvenir book of nearly 300 pictures of people and events in the 1980s.

DUNSTABLE IN DETAIL: Nigel Benson.   09509773 2 2
A hundred of the town's buildings and features, plus town trail map.

OLD DUNSTABLE: Bill Twaddle.
A new edition of this collection of early photographs.   1 871199 05 0

BOURNE and BRED: A Dunstable Boyhood Between the Wars:
Colin Bourne.
An elegantly written, well-illustrated book capturing the spirit of the town
over fifty years ago.   1 871199 40 9

ROYAL HOUGHTON: Pat Lovering: 0 9509773 1 4
Illustrated history of Houghton Regis from the earliest times to the present.

THE STOPSLEY BOOK: James Dyer.
Definitive, detailed account of this historic area of Luton. 150 rare
photographs.   h/b – 1 871199 24 7; p/b – 1 871199 04 2

THE CHANGING FACE OF LUTON: An Illustrated History:
Stephen Bunker, Robin Holgate and Marian Nichols.
Luton's development from earliest times to the present busy industrial
town. Illustrated in colour and mono.
       h/b – 1 871199 66 2; p/b – 1 871199 71 9

THE MEN WHO WORE STRAW HELMETS:
Policing Luton, 1840–1974: Tom Madigan.
Meticulously chronicled history; dozens of rare photographs; author served
in Luton Police for fifty years.   h/b – 1 871199 81 6; p/b – 1 871199 11 5

BETWEEN THE HILLS:
The Story of Lilley, a Chiltern Village:
Roy Pinnock.   1 871199 02 6
A priceless piece of our heritage – the rural beauty remains but the
customs and way of life described here have largely disappeared.

KENILWORTH SUNSET:
A Luton Town Supporter's Journal:
Tim Kingston.
Frank and funny account of football's ups and downs.   1 871199 83 2

A HATTER GOES MAD!:
Kristina Howells.   1 871199 58 1
Luton Town footballers, officials and supporters talk to a female fan.

LEGACIES: Tales and Legends of Luton and the North Chilterns:
Vic Lea.
Twenty-five mysteries and stories based on fact, including Luton Town
Football Club. Many photographs.   1 8711199 91 3

LEAFING THROUGH LITERATURE:
Writers' Lives in Hertfordshire and Bedfordshire: David Carroll.
Illustrated short biographies of many famous authors and their
connections with these counties.   1 871199 01 8

A PILGRIMAGE IN HERTFORDSHIRE: H M Alderman.
Classic, between-the-wars tour round the county, embellished with line
drawings.   1 871199 33 6

SUGAR MICE AND STICKLEBACKS:
Childhood Memories of a Hertfordshire Lad: Harry Edwards
Vivid evocation of those gentler pre-war days in an archetypal village,
Hertingfordbury.   1 871199 88 3

SWANS IN MY KITCHEN: Lis Dorer.
Story of a Swan Sanctuary near Hemel Hempstead.   1 871199 62 X

THE HILL OF THE MARTYR:
An Architectural History of St. Albans Abbey: Eileen Roberts.
Scholarly and readable chronological narrative history of Hertfordshire
and Bedfordshire's famous cathedral. Fully illustrated with photographs
and plans.   h/b – 1 871199 21 2; p/b – 1 871199 26 3

CHILTERN ARCHAEOLOGY: RECENT WORK:
A Handbook for the Next Decade:
edited by Robin Holgate.
The latest views, results and excavations by twenty-three leading
archaeologists throughout the Chilterns.   1 871199 52 2

THE TALL HITCHIN SERGEANT:
A Victorian Crime Novel Based on Fact: Edgar Newman.
Mixes real police officers and authentic background with an exciting
storyline.   1 871199 07 7

THE TALL HITCHIN INSPECTOR'S CASEBOOK:
A Victorian Crime Novel Based on Fact: Edgar Newman.
Worthies of the time encounter more archetypal villains.   1 871199 67 0

SPECIALLY FOR CHILDREN

VILLA BELOW THE KNOLLS: A Story of Roman Britain:
Michael Dundrow.
An exciting adventure for young John in Totternhoe and Dunstable two
thousand years ago.   1 871199 42 5

THE RAVENS: One Boy Against the Might of Rome:
James Dyer.   1 871199 60 3
On the Barton Hills and in the south-east of England as the men of the
great fort of Ravensburgh (near Hexton) confront the invaders.

Books Distributed by THE BOOK CASTLE

Pictorial Guide to
    Bedfordshire .... Meadows / Larkman 0900804 10 6
Old Bedfordshire .... Houfe 0900804 15 7
The Story of Bedford .... Godber 0900804 24 6
Pictorial Guide to Hertfordshire .... Meadows ...... 0900804 22 x
The Story of St. Albans .... Toms 0900804 28 9
History of Milton Keynes, vol 1 .... Markham 0900804 29 7
History of Milton Keynes, vol 2 .... Markham 0900804 30 0
Old Aylesbury .... Viney / Nightingale 0900804 21 1
Village Schooldays and Beyond,
    1906–23 .... Chapman 0951821717
Claydon .... Chapman 0951821709

Further titles are in preparation.
All the above are available via any bookshop, or from the publisher and bookseller,
THE BOOK CASTLE
12 Church Street, Dunstable, Bedfordshire, LU5 4RU
Tel: (01582) 605670